D1239363

Home Away From Home

Home to Collingsworth
Book 2

by

Kimberly Rae Jordan

A CORD OF THREE STRANDS IS NOT EASILY BROKEN.

A man, a woman & their God.
Three Strand Press publishes Christian Romance stories
that intertwine love, faith and family.
Always clean. Always heartwarming. Always uplifting.

↝ Chapter One ↜

LAUREL Collingsworth-Davis frowned as she pulled into the empty driveway of her home. Matt's truck wasn't there even though he'd planned to get off work a little early that day. Laurel climbed from her car and let herself into the garage through the side door. A quick glance revealed that his truck wasn't parked there either. Not that she had thought it might be. Once the colder weather had passed, Matt rarely parked his truck in the garage.

With a sinking feeling in the pit of her stomach, Laurel walked across the garage to the door that led to the mud room. She made her way to the kitchen and immediately spotted the note on the counter in Matt's bold handwriting.

Decided to leave early with a couple of the guys. Have a good weekend. See you Sunday night.

And that was it. No "I love you" or "I'll miss you". Laurel pressed her fingers to her forehead. She knew things were tense between them, but she hadn't thought he'd leave for two days without at least saying goodbye to her. The night before she'd told him she'd be home from work before he left. Apparently he hadn't cared to hang around.

Though things had started going downhill after Gran's funeral, this was an all-new low, and she knew it was largely her fault. But how was she supposed to tell Matt she needed him to reconsider something that had been set in stone since the beginning of their relationship? He had insisted on one condition, just one, and at the time she'd agreed to it. But now she needed him to reconsider.

With a sigh, Laurel pulled her cell phone from her pocket and texted a message to Matt.

Sorry I missed you. Had some baking to send with you. : (Hope you have a good weekend. Love you.

She didn't anticipate he'd respond since he was driving, but she knew she had to keep communicating with him. Somehow they needed to get their relationship back on track. While she couldn't imagine life without Matt; she also had other things to consider now. If he wouldn't compromise, it might well be over for them.

Laurel shuddered at the thought. Instead of doing any of her usual daily chores, she went into the bedroom and laid down on the bed. As usual, she was exhausted at the end of the day, and this week, in particular, had dragged. Though she loved her position as a home economics teacher in a private Christian school, lately it had been harder and harder for her to concentrate on her job with everything else going on. Summer break couldn't arrive soon enough. Even though the next couple of months promised to be stressful, the change of pace would still be a welcome one.

She set the alarm on her phone to make sure she didn't sleep too long, then, pulling Matt's pillow close, Laurel closed her eyes and let exhaustion override her emotions.

∽∾

Matt heard the alert for a text message. Though he didn't check his phone, he knew it was probably Laurel. He already regretted his decision to leave without talking to her, but it was too late now to turn back. Things had just been so tense between them lately he'd figured that a goodbye would have just been plain awkward. And now he was on his own for the drive since the guys who'd originally planned to ride with him had their plans change.

He was looking forward to the weekend even though he knew time apart was probably the last thing they needed. Ever since her grandmother's funeral, Laurel had been distant. And his crazy schedule hadn't helped much. Out before she was even up in the morning and not back until after sunset, lately she was often in bed and already asleep when he got home. They hadn't had a decent conversation in what felt like weeks, and their physical time together was non-existent. He missed what they'd once had, but he didn't know what he needed to do to get back to that point. Though he'd asked her what was wrong a few times, she'd just brushed aside his questions.

If anything, they should be having a great time right now. Financially, they were set for life thanks to her grandmother's will. He knew they'd both continue to work because they loved their jobs, but they wouldn't have to worry about finances any more. Of course, that was assuming all the sisters showed up at the appointed time for their month together. He knew Jessa would be there, and Violet had seemed committed as well. The only loose cannon was Cami.

He and Laurel hadn't spent a lot of time talking about their pasts. When they first started dating, she'd told him she'd rather focus on the present and future. Given his own past, Matt had been more than willing to agree to that. But now he wondered how things had been for those girls growing up. It hadn't seemed to have had a big impact on Laurel. She was level-headed and, for lack of a better word, normal. Nothing in the year they'd dated or the two years since they'd married had shown him anything different.

But something had certainly flipped a switch in his wife since the funeral. He had no idea what it was, and part of him was scared to press too hard for an answer.

The alarm pulled Laurel from a deep sleep. She lay for

several minutes trying to orientate herself. There was still light peeking around the edges of the curtains, but Matt's side of the bed hadn't been slept in. She rolled to her back and covered her eyes with her arm. All she wanted to do was go back to sleep, but as the fogginess of sleep wore off, she remembered why she had set her alarm.

She sat up more quickly than she should have, and the room spun for a couple of seconds. Once the room stopped moving, Laurel got up and changed into something more comfortable before going downstairs to wait for Violet. She'd been surprised, and pleased, when Violet had phoned to see if she could stay with her for two nights. She, Dean and Addy were coming to the Twin Cities to visit his parents, and Violet had thought it best she stay with Laurel.

Laurel was happy to have her visit since Matt was gone anyway. As she waited for them to arrive, she pulled out some of the baking she'd set aside for Matt and put it on a plate. Violet had said to expect her around eight-thirty. Since they hadn't left Collingsworth until after five, it would be late by the time they made it to the Twin Cities. Dean planned to drop Violet off at Laurel's first, and then the next morning he'd pick her up to go meet his parents.

It was almost nine by the time the doorbell rang. Laurel pushed up from the couch where she'd been watching television. It wasn't just Violet on her front step though. Addy stood at her side, and Dean came up the steps with a bag in his hand.

"C'mon in, guys," Laurel said and stepped back to let them into the house.

Violet gave her a quick hug. "Thanks for letting me stay here this weekend."

"It's my pleasure. Matt's gone, so it will just be us girls." Laurel smiled at the young girl holding Violet's hand. "How are you, Addy?"

"I'm good!" The wide grin on the little girl's face backed up her statement.

"Are you glad school's almost out?" Laurel waved for

keep Rose from you if you wanted to claim her as your own. And I would certainly support that. I think she needs you."

Laurel blinked back tears. "But how do I explain why I've never told her who I was before this? And what do I tell Matt? Because the thing is, it's not just Rose that's an issue here."

"What do you mean?" Violet shifted to sit sideways on the couch, her feet tucked under her.

Laurel took a deep breath and pressed a hand to her stomach, bracing herself to say the words that had only been playing around in her head for the past four weeks. "I'm pregnant."

❦ Chapter Two ❧

VIOLET'S jaw dropped. "Oh my."

"Yeah...oh my." Laurel's shoulders slumped. "I don't know what I'm going to do."

"Weren't you guys taking precautions? Especially considering Matt's stance on not having kids? Wouldn't he have taken permanent steps to prevent it from happening?"

"He tried to, but most doctors weren't willing to do anything given his age. They all said he'd change his mind and that a reversal would be difficult. So I was on the pill, but I didn't realize going on antibiotics can impact the effectiveness of the birth control. I was on them three times in the months before Gran's funeral."

"Wow. Just...wow." Violet stared at her, a stunned look on her face, but slowly it faded and a small smile played on her lips. "But you know, I'm going to say this. Congratulations!" She flung her arms around Laurel. "I know the circumstances are difficult, but I feel this baby is something special. I know all babies are special, but I think God has a reason for giving you this child. This brings to mind a verse I read the other day. It talked about how man plans his way, but the Lord directs his path. Sounds like you guys had plans, but the Lord has another path for you. Trust Him."

Laurel sat in her sister's embrace and for a moment let all the worries about Rose and Matt slide away, and she found that in her heart, she was truly happy about the baby growing inside her. A little life made up of bits of her and Matt. A physical manifestation of the love they had for each other. If only Matt felt the same way. Would he make her choose?

Tears slid down her cheeks. Would she have to give up one love to keep the other? She turned and buried her face in Violet's shoulder. She heard Violet murmuring, but couldn't make out the words. It didn't matter though; the comfort offered by her sister was just what she needed.

When Laurel finally sat back, she rubbed her hands across her eyes. "Sorry for crying all over you."

Violet shook her head. "Don't apologize. I'm glad I could be here for you. I just wish I knew how to help you and Matt. But for now, just know that if you ever need to talk, you give me a call. And I won't be telling anyone about what you've told me here tonight. I'm so happy and excited, but it's your news to share."

"I'd love to share it, but first I have to figure out what to tell Matt about Rose and the baby."

"I know you'll do what's right. I'll be praying for you," Violet assured her. "And now that you've shared your secret, I have something to share too."

"You and Dean are engaged?" Laurel asked with a smile.

Violet shook her head. "That hasn't happened. Yet!" She grinned, but then sobered quickly. "I've been looking for Mama."

"Mama?" Of all the things Laurel had expected her to say, that hadn't even been on the radar. "What about her?"

"I've hired a private investigator to try to find her, or find out what happened to her." Violet drew her legs up, wrapping her arms around them. "I had wondered for years where she was, but any time I asked Gran about it, she shut me down."

"That doesn't surprise me," Laurel admitted. "She really didn't want her to be part of our lives."

"Dean helped me find someone who was willing to look for her."

"Have they been able to find out anything?"

Violet frowned, her brows drawing together. "Not as much as I had hoped. Tom—he's the guy helping me—told me a few weeks back he wasn't sure Mama was even still alive."

That statement impacted Laurel more than she would have thought it would. The woman was virtually a stranger to her. She could meet her on a street and not know who she was. "Why would he think that?"

"A guy was with her when she came to drop Lily off. Tom discovered he is also missing. Hasn't been seen or heard from since that time either. It's like they both dropped off the face of the earth."

"But he hasn't been able to find out for sure something like that happened to her, has he?"

"No," Violet said with a shake of her head. "But I know he's not holding out a lot of hope."

"I'm sorry," Laurel said. "I know you were closest to her of all of us."

"Yes, I was. I always knew this might be the outcome given the life she led, but I guess I had hoped for something different." She paused and caught her lower lip between her teeth. "There is something else."

Laurel lifted a brow at Violet. "You're full of secrets tonight, aren't you?"

"You don't know the half of it." Violet sighed. "Tom discovered something else while gathering information on Mama. Some of the people mentioned her being pregnant."

"When wasn't she pregnant?" Laurel asked drily. "It seemed every time she turned around she was having another kid."

"That's the thing. The dates people have given Tom for this pregnancy don't line up with any of us."

Laurel frowned. "Do you think she miscarried? Or is there another sibling somewhere out there?"

Violet's forehead furrowed. "I don't know. But from what Tom said, it sounded like people knew her near the end of the pregnancy. So I'm inclined to say another sibling...possibly a boy."

"A boy? Why a boy?"

"Because if it had been a girl, Gran would have kept her. After all, she went on to keep Lily."

"So you think she just abandoned the boy?" Laurel asked as she laid a hand over her abdomen.

"No, actually, I don't. A boy would carry on the Collingsworth name. I think perhaps she gave him to someone to raise. To take care of him until...I'm not sure what."

Laurel shook her head. "I have a hard time believing any of this. Have you run this past your detective guy?"

"Yes, and he said it was a possibility."

"And Dean?"

Violet tilted her head and wrinkled her nose. "Dean isn't so sure. I think he just doesn't want to believe Gran would do something like that."

"Well, frankly, I don't want to believe that either," Laurel informed her.

"I know but Gran and her secrets." Violet gave her head a shake. "It's hard not to consider the possibility."

They sat chatting for a bit longer then Violet said she needed to get to bed. "No sleeping in for me tomorrow. I think we're going to the zoo or maybe the Mall of America. I'm figuring Addy will make that decision."

"Well, make yourself at home. There's plenty of food in the fridge. I'll try to be up before you leave, but no promises."

Violet smiled and hugged Laurel again. "Don't worry about getting up with me. I'll see you tomorrow night."

Once Violet had gone to bed, Laurel shut off the lights and locked up before retreating to the master bedroom. She sat on the edge of the bed, staring at the floor. It was becoming very difficult for her to concentrate on just one thing and make a decision. She felt like she faced a domino effect with the issues at hand. Making the wrong decision for just one of them would set off a negative reaction with all the rest.

She pressed a hand to her stomach. Because her intimate times with Matt had been more limited than usual over the past few months, Laurel could pinpoint almost exactly when conception had occurred. By her own calculations, she was just over two months along. Though she had a little more time before the pregnancy became too obvious, she wouldn't be able to hide her growing stomach forever. And it was only because of Matt's horrendous schedule lately that she'd been able to hide it as much as she had.

Morning sickness had been plaguing her, sending her running to the bathroom at seven each morning like clockwork. Thankfully, Matt was long gone by that point so didn't witness her throwing up. On the days he was home, she made sure to go to the bathroom down the hall while he slept in so he wouldn't hear her. But somehow she had to figure out how to tell the man who had been adamant about not having any children, that he was going to have not just one, but two, added to his life.

Laurel stood and went to the chair where Matt had left the t-shirt he'd worn to bed the night before. She picked it up and buried her face in the soft cotton fabric. He'd showered before bed so the scent of the male body wash he used still lingered. The muscles of her throat tightened as she inhaled the familiar scent. She carried the shirt the bathroom and after changing out of her clothes, slipped it on. As she lay under the covers in bed a few minutes later, Laurel felt hot tears slip down her cheeks. Alone in the dark, she finally admitted to herself just how scared she was about the way things were going.

"I need you to know that I'm really serious about this," Matt said, his expression every bit as severe as his tone. *"I don't want you to say you agree, all the while thinking you'll change your, or my, mind later on. I do not want to have children. That is set in stone for me. If it's not the same for you, then we might as well not go any further."*

The hard determination in his voice surprised Laurel. Clearly this was something he'd thought a lot about. "Do you mind me asking why?"

Matt's gaze slipped from hers. "Let's just say I've had a few experiences in my lifetime that have convinced me there are already plenty of children in this world. I don't need to add to them. I just know that for me, having children is not something I want. I need to know that anyone I'm with will feel the same way. If my stand on this means I never marry, I'm okay with that too." He met her gaze again. *"So please, do us both a favor...if you're hoping to have children someday, walk away from me now. It will be much harder to let you go later if you change your mind, but I will. That's how strongly I feel about this."*

Laurel shuddered at the memory. At the time, she had had no problem accepting Matt's stipulation for their relationship and later their marriage. She'd honestly felt she didn't deserve to be a mother. If she'd been any sort of mother at all, she would have stood up to Gran. Instead, she'd gone along with everything the older woman had suggested even though her heart was breaking.

But what was she going to do now? When she finally got up the nerve to tell Matt, would she end up a single mother of two children? Financially it wouldn't be the hardship it might have been without the inheritance, but losing Matt...

Her phone's ring tone jerked her from her depressing thoughts. She picked it up, her heart skipping a beat at the sight of Matt's name on the display. Even though he couldn't see her, she swiped her hand across her cheeks to wipe away the tears as she answered the phone.

"Hi," Matt said in response to her greeting. "How's it going?"

"It's going fine," Laurel replied, hating the stilted distance of their conversations these days. "How is the retreat? Is there a good turnout?"

"It's going pretty good. I'd say there's about thirty to forty guys here." Laurel heard him yawn. "I'm tired though. Just wanted to say goodnight before I turned in."

"Yes, I'm sure it's been a long day for you since you were up so early. Hope you sleep well tonight."

"I'm sure I will. The beds look half-way decent. Although I'd probably sleep fine on a slab of rock given how tired I am."

Laurel wanted the conversation to go on. She missed him. She missed how things used to be. "Okay. Well, I won't keep you up."

There was a beat of silence on Matt's end of the call before he said, "Yeah, no sleeping in tomorrow, so I'd better get what sleep I can."

"Have a good night." Laurel paused then added, "I love you."

"You too," Matt said. "I'll try to call again tomorrow some time." They said good night, and then the call was over.

Clutching the phone close, Laurel rolled to her side and drew her legs up. Pain ate at her heart like acid. Though she knew the initial distance between them had been her fault, the longer it drew out, the more unbearable it became. She hadn't been able to really share all the emotions she was feeling about Gran's passing. There was the anger she'd never fully let go of because of what had happened with Rose, and now the regret that she and Gran hadn't been able to work through their differences. Dealing with those on her own had been the first crack in the closeness she shared with Matt. And just as she had pulled away initially, he was pulling away now.

Laurel didn't know how to get that closeness back, not

when the news she still had to share with him hung over their relationship like a guillotine. He might have been able to accept Rose since she had already been born, but this new baby growing inside her...that was a different story completely. And there was nothing she could—or would—do to change that.

Matt sat on the edge of the bed he'd claimed for the duration of the retreat, the phone clasped in his hands. He braced his elbows on his knees and bent his head until it pressed the edge of the phone. Calling Laurel had been a mistake. He should have texted her to say goodnight, because the call had just emphasized the distance between them. There was something wrong. He knew it, because he knew Laurel that well. But instead of sharing with him, she was hiding it. Ever since her grandmother had passed away she'd been subdued and introspective in a way she never had been around him before.

She had been a soft-spoken, quiet woman when they'd met. He'd liked that about her. She didn't just chatter on endlessly about things. When she talked it was because she had something important to say. As they had gotten to know each other, she'd begun to open up and talk more with him about things of lesser importance. And he'd like that about her too. It felt like she was sharing parts of herself with him that she'd never shared with anyone else. She'd quickly become his best friend, and she had said he was hers.

But something had happened in the past couple of months that had changed things. She wasn't sharing much of anything with him anymore, which made the conversation they'd just had almost painful. They weren't good at small talk when there were big things that weren't being discussed.

Part of him wondered if she had found out something about his past. When they'd started dating, she'd asked about it periodically, but soon she'd figured out it was something he wasn't going to discuss. He told her it hadn't been a happy time and that, like her, he preferred to focus on the present and the future. Unfortunately right now, their present wasn't too happy and who knew what the future held.

A hand landed on his shoulder. "Everything okay, man?"

Matt looked up to see his friend, Devon, standing beside him. "I hope so. Laurel's kind of turned off the communication since her grandmother's death. I'm not sure what's going on."

Devon sat down next to him. "Were they close?"

"That's the strange thing. They weren't. I mean, one of the reasons we eloped was because she didn't want to have to deal with her family and a wedding." Matt turned his phone over and over in his hands. "When I ask her what's wrong, she just brushes it aside. She was really sick for a few weeks before the funeral and has used that as an excuse. She's tired, doesn't want to talk."

"I know it can be alarming when a woman decides to stop talking in a relationship, but maybe she's just trying to work through her feelings regarding her grandmother's death."

"I hope so." Matt shrugged. "I'm at a loss as to how to deal with it."

"Just love her through it, man," Devon suggested. "For better or worse, right?"

Matt nodded. "Yes. I just never thought something like this would come up with us, you know? We've always seemed to be so in sync. I can count on one hand the number of fights we've had since getting married. Which, given my past, is amazing. But this isn't even like a fight...it's just dead air."

"Do you think you should go back?" Devon asked.

"No. Her sister is in town with her boyfriend for the weekend and is staying with Laurel. It would just make it more awkward if we're trying to work on stuff." Matt stretched out his legs. "I have a feeling being here will do me more good than being there."

"Well, it's certainly something we can pray about this weekend. I think most of us married guys have dealt with this a time or two. You can get through it; you just have to be patient and understanding. And whatever you do, fight the urge to back off as well." Devon gave his head a shake. "Worst thing I ever did the first time Amy and I had something like this crop up. In the end it made things much worse than if I'd just continued to be there for her without trying to pressure her or to protect myself."

Matt winced at Devon's words. He knew he was already guilty of this. Fear was telling him to brace for the worst, to protect himself from the pain that was to come. He'd never had anything as good in his life as his relationship with Laurel, and he was afraid it wasn't going to last. He certainly didn't deserve her, but he'd do anything to keep her. Anything except have kids.

"Well, I'm going to go give Amy a call and then head for bed." Devon stood and laid a hand on his shoulder. "If you want to talk again tomorrow, let me know."

Matt looked up and gave him a halfhearted smile. "Thanks. I appreciate it."

Once his friend left him, he opened his duffle bag and pulled out his pajama bottoms and a t-shirt and headed for the bathroom that was shared by the two bedrooms in the cabin. He and Devon shared the one bedroom and a couple of other guys shared the other. The cabin also had a sitting area, but no kitchen. They would be having all their meals in the main building with the other men at the retreat. He had been looking forward to this all week, had actually been anticipating being away from the tension in the home he and Laurel shared, but now that he was here, he wanted to be with her.

Even though they'd been distant recently, Matt found he missed Laurel with a very real physical ache in his heart. He longed to wrap his arms around her and pull her softness close to him, to inhale the scent of her shampoo. It had been too long since they shared such an embrace. A week was too long...and it had been several weeks now. Even in their bed, the time they used to spend talking was gone now because she was usually asleep by the time he crawled into bed. When he would wake in the morning, he'd find her curled on her side, facing away from him.

Matt sucked in a deep breath then let it out. There was nothing he could do about that tonight, but when he got home on Sunday he would put Devon's advice into action. Hopefully he could reverse any damage he'd done already and let Laurel know he was there for her, whatever it was that was bothering her.

Laurel didn't have much time to visit with Violet the next evening as Dean didn't drop her off until close to ten. She'd woken sick again that morning, and it had just dragged on all day, which had been unusual. She ended up spending most of Saturday in bed. Sunday morning she got up to say goodbye to Violet before she left, then, after a short debate with herself about church, went back to bed.

Matt hadn't called Saturday night though he had sent a text late to say good night. She knew she was slipping into depression, overwhelmed by the decisions that faced her and the potential impact they would have on her life. The only other time she'd felt like this had been in the month following Rose's birth and her gran's departure with her baby. She and Cami had stayed behind in the special boarding school they'd been sent to when Gran had figured out she was pregnant. Back then she'd wanted to retreat from the world. And now all she wanted to do was crawl into bed and sleep. So she did.

The silence that met Matt when he walked into the house concerned him. "Laurel?"

He dropped his bag on the floor next to the door, and headed for the kitchen. Dirty dishes sat on the counter, but the air held no aroma of anything having been cooked recently. It was unlike Laurel to leave things undone. She had to be home, unless a friend had picked her up, since her car was in the driveway.

There was no sign of her in the living room, so he made

his way to their bedroom. The door was slightly ajar, but heavy curtains pulled over the windows kept it dark. He flicked the switch that turned on the two lights on the wall on either side of their bed. Their soft illumination revealed a lump on the mattress.

His concern morphed into alarm as he walked further into the room. Laurel was curled up under the covers, facing toward the middle of the bed. He toed off his shoes and walked around to the other side. The bed shifted as he stretched out on it. Laurel moved a bit but didn't open her eyes. Even in the dim light he could see the pallor of her complexion. He wondered if there was something more wrong than the bad flu bug she'd had a couple of months back. It seemed she'd never completely recovered from that.

He reached out and brushed the hair from her face. "Laurel?"

She moved then, her eyes opening slowly. She blinked a couple of times before pushing herself up into a sitting position. "Matt? What time is it?"

He glanced at the clock on her side of the bed. "Almost five."

"In the afternoon?" She drew her legs in and brushed the hair back from her cheek. Disorientation seemed to still cloud her thoughts.

"Yes. I just got back from the retreat." Matt watched as she blinked rapidly as if to clear her vision. "Are you okay? What's going on?"

"I laid down to take a nap. I guess I slept longer than I'd planned."

Matt frowned. "A nap? You don't look like you even got dressed today. Didn't you go to church?"

She let out an audible sigh, and her shoulders slumped. She tugged at the fabric of the sheet pooled in her lap. "I got up when Violet left, but then I was still tired so I came back to bed."

Matt shifted to the middle of the bed and leaned back

against the pillows. He reached out and gave Laurel's arm a gentle tug. She glanced at him over her shoulder then turned to curl against his side, her head resting on his chest.

He wanted to pelt her with questions, demand she tell him what was wrong, but keeping in mind the advice he'd received over the weekend, Matt just held her. Her body was stiff against him at first, but soon he felt her softening. She lifted her leg and rested it along his thigh and laid her hand on his chest. It was a familiar position, one they'd shared often, but not recently. He closed his eyes and let out a deep sigh. He'd missed this so much.

"I missed you," he said although he hadn't planned to voice the feeling.

"I missed you too," Laurel replied, her voice soft.

He wanted more right then, to do more than just hold her, but he held back. There was still something between them that overrode whatever physical intimacy they may have been feeling at that moment. But at least this gave him hope. She hadn't outright rejected him, so perhaps what she was dealing with had little to do with him.

❧ Chapter Three ❧

LAUREL kept her eyes squeezed shut. Lying with Matt this way was a clear reminder of what she had to lose if the worst happened. Tears pricked at her eyes, but the last thing she wanted was to start crying. Matt hadn't pressed for a reason as to why she was still in bed, but most definitely he'd want an explanation if she started to cry. This pregnancy, in addition to making her tired and sick, was making her much more emotional than usual. Matt knew she rarely cried, so to find her in tears now would no doubt alarm him.

They lay there for a while, neither talking, but when her stomach rumbled, Matt asked, "Hungry?"

Laurel shifted away from him to sit up. "Yeah. I guess I haven't eaten yet today."

"How about I order in?" Matt suggested. "What are you in the mood for?"

Laurel sat for a moment, trying to figure out if there was something in particular her pregnant stomach was craving. "Pizza?"

"Sounds good to me."

She felt the bed shift as Matt moved. Knowing she needed

to get up as well, Laurel swung her legs over the bed and slowly stood, hoping to avoid the room spinning this time. She didn't hear any movement from Matt, so glanced in his direction.

He stood on his side of the bed watching her. "You're wearing my shirt."

Laurel glanced down. She'd forgotten she wore his shirt after having put it on that first night he was away. As she met his gaze again, her breath caught. At one time the look in his eye would have meant a little more time spent in bed together, but today he blinked and it was gone. "Yes. I missed you."

"I'm glad." The corner of Matt's mouth lifted in a half smile, and he winked at her. "If I wouldn't have gotten some strange looks from the guys at the retreat, I might have considered wearing one of yours."

Laurel got a mental image of Matt in one of her t-shirts and couldn't stop the chuckle that came as a result. It was a weird feeling to laugh since it was something she'd done very little of late. She sobered quickly though, and stood, hands clenched in front of her, thankful for the looseness of the shirt so nothing of her swelling belly was visible. She felt in that moment of closeness she owed Matt...something.

"Listen, I know I've been a little off lately," she began. Matt gave a slight nod. "I just...I'm just having to work through a few things."

"Things you can't share with me?" Matt asked, concern clear on his face.

"Not yet. Some of it has come about as a result of Gran's death. There are things you don't know about my family. Just like there are things I don't know about yours. Her death brought up a lot of stuff I need to deal with."

Matt tilted his head, his gaze serious. "And that's all it is? Nothing more?"

It was a wonderful thing to have someone know you so well when the relationship was going great, but it also meant they could read you in the bad times too. Part of her wanted to spill everything in that moment, but there was also a chance things could change. Maybe in talking with Jessa, she'd feel it was better to leave things as they were with Rose. Laurel still wasn't one hundred percent convinced she was the best mother for Rose anyway, but if Jessa thought they should tell Rose the truth, she would do it. And the pregnancy was still in those first few months where a miscarriage could occur. So for now... "That's most of it. You know how it is when things stress me out in one area of my life; it tends to bleed over into others too."

Matt didn't reply right away, and just as he knew her well, she knew him. She could tell he wasn't completely buying what she was selling. He was battling whether to press her or not, she could see that. Relief flooded her when he nodded.

"I'll go place that order now," he said as he walked toward the bedroom door.

Alone in the room, Laurel pressed her hands to her stomach. "I can't tell him about you just yet, little one. Hang in there."

Whether it had been the abundance of sleep she'd had over the weekend or the conversation with Matt, Laurel felt more like herself than she had in weeks. As she stood in the bathroom brushing her hair, she felt hope. She wasn't sure why, but something was making her feel like maybe things could truly work out. She knew Matt loved her, just as she loved him. She just hoped it would be enough when everything came to light.

When she got home from school the next afternoon, she decided it was time to talk to Jessa about Rose. Matt wasn't due home for a few hours, so it would be a good time to broach the subject. Up until last night she just hadn't felt like she was in a good place to have a discussion with Jessa on the subject. Talking with Jessa at the best of times could be stressful for her.

When her older sister answered her call, she said, "Hi Jessa. It's Laurel."

"Hey! How's it going?" Jessa asked.

"It's going. Is this a good time to talk?"

There was a brief pause. "About?"

Laurel took a deep breath and blew it out. "Rose."

"Yes. It's a good time. She's at her friend's house for the afternoon."

"I know I probably should have called sooner about this..."

"It's okay. I figured you'd call me when the time was right," Jessa assured her.

"I was surprised Gran didn't leave anything in her will about it." Laurel sat down in the rocker by the front window so she could see if Matt arrived home early. She knew she'd taken a chance not telling Matt about it before the reading of the will, but she'd counted on Gran's desire for privacy to make sure it was only the girls present for any sort of discussion pertaining to Rose and Lily.

"She did, actually," Jessa said.

Laurel straightened. "She did? Why didn't Stan say anything about it?"

"I asked him not to. I wasn't sure what Matt knew about the situation, so didn't want it to come out of the blue if he was unaware of who Rose was."

"Yeah, I haven't told him yet," Laurel admitted.

"I thought that might be the case. I knew Gran had scared us all into silence over it, so I was pretty sure you wouldn't have told Matt yet."

"I just figured there was no sense in upsetting things. I thought Gran would be around for years. At least until Rose was of legal age when it wouldn't matter anymore if I told her who I really was."

"I didn't know if Gran had changed anything again with regards to the guardianship of either Rose or Lily before her death," Jessa said. "About three years ago, she had me added as a guardian for them both. I've been the one taking care of them for the last few years. I do all the school and doctor stuff. So I wasn't sure if she'd changed that in her will or not."

"I didn't realize that," Laurel said. "Of course I wasn't privy to much considering, unlike with us sisters, she actually adopted Rose."

"Yes, I actually didn't know that until recently. In all those years, I just assumed Rose's arrangement was the same as ours. I only found out when I talked to Stan. He told me she'd made changes shortly before her death. They did affect you, but I didn't want to press you into something you weren't ready for, so I just told Stan that for the time being, things would continue on as normal."

"So you're still a guardian for Rose?"

"Yes. But Gran changed it and added you as a guardian for her as well and also added Violet for Lily. Just to have a backup in case something ever happened to me. Of course, in Lily's situation that's not such a big deal as she's just months from being legal. Rose, however, still requires a long term guardian."

"Yes, I know, that's why I wanted to talk to you."

"Do you want to tell her you're her mother?" Jessa's question was blunt and to the point.

Unfortunately, Laurel didn't have a straight answer. "I want to know what you think is best. You know her state of mind."

"Well, actually, I think more important is how Matt feels about this. Is he willing to take on a ten year old daughter?"

Laurel sighed. "I guess Violet didn't tell you?"

"About what?"

"Before we got married, Matt told me he didn't want children. That was non-negotiable. If I wanted them at any point in my future, then things wouldn't work out for us. I assured him I was okay not having children, because back then I was. I figured I'd had my one chance to be a mother and had failed miserably."

"So why are you even asking me about taking Rose?" Anger laced Jessa's tone. "I won't have her go to a home where one parent doesn't want her around."

"Because it doesn't matter whether or not Rose is here, Matt's going to become a father."

Laurel heard Jessa's quick intake of breath. "You're pregnant?"

"Yes."

"How far along? How did it happen? Have you told Matt?" Jessa fired the questions like bullets from a gun.

"I'm around two months. No, I haven't told Matt, and ask Violet for the details of how it came about." Laurel swallowed hard. "Basically if Matt hasn't changed his mind about becoming a parent, I will be raising both Rose and the baby on my own."

"So why do you want Rose if you will already had a baby to care for?"

"Because she's mine. I have had to love her from a distance for too long. Now I have the chance to be the mother to her I should had been. I want her. But...I realize that might not be the best thing for her. I don't want to uproot her from her life, although if the worst happens, I might be coming back to Collingsworth regardless."

"I'm sorry this has gotten so mixed up," Jessa said. "I never would have guessed that about Matt. Why doesn't he want children?"

"To be honest, I'm not entirely sure. He gave me some reasons, but I've always wondered if there was more. Up until Gran's death and this pregnancy, I was okay with his position and didn't need to know why he was so set against kids. But once Gran passed, I realized that I needed—wanted—to step up and take responsibility for Rose. And then the pregnancy...I'm just really scared it's not going to make a difference. That no matter how much he loves me, whatever has set him so adamantly against children will be stronger than our love."

"When do you plan to tell him?" Jessa's tone had softened.

"I'm not sure. I keep putting it off because I don't want to...lose him. I know time is ticking with the pregnancy. He's going to notice things sooner or later. With Rose, I will probably tell him at the same time, but I won't have her come live with me if you feel strongly she would be better to stay where there at the manor."

"I'll be honest. I don't really want her to be in a situation that's got a lot of upheaval. If you and Matt are fighting or not getting along because of this, I'd rather she not be around that. But if Matt agrees, I'd say it would be good for her to have a family with a mom and dad, not just sisters."

"Okay. I think I'm going to have to wait until school is out to tell Matt. If I tell him now and things fall apart, I still have to finish the school year, and it's already hard enough just dealing with the stuff that's come with the pregnancy. I don't want to have to deal with my life falling apart at the same time."

"Try to think positively, Laurel," Jessa encouraged her. "I know it's tempting to try to prepare for the worst, but I'll be praying, and I know Violet will be too, that God will have changed Matt's heart with regards to having children."

"Thank you. I'm praying He has too, but I'm afraid to broach the subject with him." She rubbed her forehead. "It's just another week until school's out. I'll tell him as soon as I'm done for the year. Then, if he doesn't take it well, I can come to Collingsworth a little early."

"We'll just trust God to prepare his heart. Remember that even when things seem darkest, God is still in control. Don't doubt that."

"Thanks, Jess."

"I've got to run and pick Rose up from her friend's, but be sure to call and let me know if something else comes up."

"I will," Laurel assured her. She hung up the phone feeling a little more settled. At least Jessa wasn't opposed to her stepping into the role as Rose's mother. An image of the little girl filled her mind, and Laurel smiled. It had been so hard not to mother Rose each time she'd seen her. In the end, it had been easier to just stay away. But now...now she finally had a shot at being a mother to her darling little girl.

And Jessa's encouragement had given her hope that even as all this was unfolding, God was preparing Matt's heart for what was to come. Surely God wouldn't give her a baby and then not change Matt's feelings about having children. Jessa was right; she had to think positively about all this.

The next morning started off cloudy, and by lunch time, they were in the midst of a torrential downpour. Laurel knew that meant most likely Matt would be home early. Because he worked construction, the rain often ended the work day if they were doing outside work. She was pretty sure he had been, so wasn't surprised to see his truck in the driveway when she got home from school.

"Rain ended my day early," Matt said as he greeted her at the door with a kiss. "Fancy a trip to the mall and then some dinner?"

It felt so...normal. Laurel didn't hesitate to agree. "Just let me change."

What Laurel hadn't counted on at the mall was being drawn to all the children's shops and baby sections in the stores. The only times she'd gone into those sections previously had been for gifts for friends or to buy clothes to send Rose for her birthday or Christmas. But now she had an ache to look through all the wonderfully small baby items. It took all she had to stick close to Matt and pretend interest in the stores she normally liked.

It was a relief when they finally left the mall and went to the Italian restaurant they both liked. As long as Laurel compartmentalized her feelings, she was able to carry on a normal conversation with Matt over dinner. She kept her thoughts from Rose and the baby, and focused on her husband. Oh, how she longed for the day when all three could share the thoughts in her head and the love in her heart.

As they were finishing their meal, Matt's phone rang. He glanced at the number and frowned. Laurel watched as he stared at the number for a long moment before answering it. Having never seen him respond like that to a call before, her curiosity was roused.

"What's up?" Matt said when he put the phone to his ear. His frown deepened as he listened to the person on the other end of the phone. "Where are you?" He closed his eyes and let out a deep sigh. "Okay, I'll be there as soon as I can."

The waitress approached them with the bill. Laurel took it from her and got money from her wallet to cover it plus a tip. She had just laid it on the table when Matt lowered the phone and tapped the screen to end the call.

"Who was that?" Laurel asked. "Is everything okay?"

"It was my brother, Steven," Matt said, his voice tight. Laurel could also see something more than just a frown on his face. Anger burned in his eyes as he put his phone away. "We need to go."

"I didn't know you had a brother," Laurel commented as she slid out of her side of the booth. She picked up her purse and looped the strap over her shoulder.

"Right now I wish I didn't," Matt said. He laid his hand on her lower back and guided her through the restaurant to the door. "His wife is in the hospital. I need to go see them. Do you want me to drop you off at home?"

Heck, no, was what Laurel wanted to say, but instead she shook her head and said, "I'll go with you. It sounds important that you get there right away."

Matt gave a single nod of his head, but didn't say anything more during the drive to the hospital. Laurel was left with a ton of questions, but didn't think right then was the time to voice them. Seriously angry vibes radiated off Matt, which didn't make much sense to her.

❧ Chapter Four ❧

EVEN though he seemed to be seething with more anger than she'd ever seen before, he still drove safely to the hospital and took care with her getting out of the truck. Once in the hospital however, he seemed to move with a single purpose, almost as if he'd forgotten about her. Laurel followed behind him as he asked for directions to where his brother and wife were.

When they got to the waiting area, Matt turned to her. "Wait here, please." Then he disappeared around the corner.

Laurel settled into one of the seats in the nearly empty waiting room. Concern weighed on her for Matt. She'd never seen him like this in three years they'd been together. And why hadn't he ever told her he had a brother? Yes, she hadn't told him about Rose, but that was a bit different. He knew all about her siblings. Early on he'd just said he didn't have contact with his mother, and his father was dead. No mention at all of siblings.

Matt suddenly reappeared, a man who looked quite like him in his wake. Once in the waiting area, her husband rounded on the man.

"What were you thinking? How could you have done this?" Matt demanded, his voice low and tight with anger.

Laurel had never seen such fury on her husband's face before. His fists were clenched, and she actually wondered if he was going to haul off and hit his brother.

"I couldn't help it. She just pushed me too far," the other man responded with a shrug. "I told her to back off. She didn't."

"So you *hit* her?" Matt took a step closer to his brother. They were about the same height, but Matt definitely had more muscle than Steven. "How could you do that? Or is this not the first time?"

Steven's fists came up, and Laurel gasped, fearful of what he might do. It sounded like maybe it wouldn't be the first punch he'd thrown that night.

"You know how women can be," Steven said. "Don't tell me you haven't thrown a punch or two. Lord knows you had some killer moves before."

Matt's jaw clenched, and he took a deep breath. "You are lower than low, man. You're as bad as he was."

Steven's fist shot out then and clipped Matt on the chin. Laurel scrambled from her seat as Matt responded with a punch to his brother's gut. "Back off, Steven. You can't win with me."

With a laugh, Steven sneered at Matt. "Wow! You punch like a girl. That didn't hurt at all. Guess you've lost your edge."

"Shut up. Just shut up. You'd better be glad I pulled that punch. And when the cops get here, you'd better come clean."

"You'd love to see me in jail, wouldn't you?"

"For this? Definitely!" Matt replied.

"It's not gonna happen. She won't press charges," Steven said with a smug look. "She knows what side her bread is buttered on."

"Why did you call me?" Matt stepped closer to his brother

again. "If this is your attitude, why did you call me? I thought you wanted help, but it's clear that's not anything you're interested in."

"I thought you'd understand. That you'd back me up." Steven shrugged. "Call it a moment of weakness."

Laurel could see the incredulous expression on Matt's face as he said, "You're an idiot. You really think I'd back you up when you've been beating on your wife? Given our past, you really thought that?"

A couple of police officers came around the corner into the waiting room. "Steven Foster?"

Laurel wondered at the different last name as she watched Matt back off and gesture to his brother.

"We understand you brought your wife in," one of the officers said.

"Yes, she fell," Steven said without blinking an eye.

"We were called because the injuries she presented with seemed to be more in line with a beating than a fall. Care to elaborate?"

Steven shrugged again. "What did she say?"

"That she fell." The officer's tone said it all, even though he continued with, "But we all know how this goes."

Steven glanced at Matt. The cops must have caught the look, because they turned to him. "And you are?"

Matt shoved his hands into the pockets of his jeans. "I'm Matt Davis. His brother."

"And do you have anything to add?" one of the officer's asked.

Laurel held her breath, wondering if blood would prove thicker than water.

"He hit her," Matt said without hesitation. "He just told me he did."

Steven lunged at him and once again managed to land a blow before the officers pulled him away. Matt didn't return the punch this time. He just stepped back.

Once they had Steven under control, one of the officers turned to Matt again. "Perhaps you could have a talk with your sister-in-law. Based on what we've seen here tonight, we're going to be arresting your brother."

"Melly wouldn't want to press charges. You can't arrest me," Steven said indignantly.

The officer holding him said, "Actually, sir, your wife has no say over whether or not charges are pressed. We make the determination if it appears likely that domestic violence has occurred. You can plead your case before the judge."

Laurel winced at the stream of swear words that came out of Steven's mouth. Matt, however, didn't even flinch. Watching all this unfold left Laurel with a ton of questions regarding Matt's past. She wondered if he'd volunteer any information or if she'd had to ask him about it.

The officers left with Steven who was still cursing about them, his wife and Matt. Laurel sank back onto her seat, not sure what to do. She would just follow Matt's lead. He stood with his back to her, and she saw his shoulders rise and fall as he took a deep breath. Then he turned around and looked at her. Though she could still see the turmoil in his eyes, the fierce anger she'd witnessed earlier was gone.

He walked to where she sat. "Let's go."

"Don't you want to talk to your sister-in-law?"

Matt shook his head. "She'll go to her grave protecting him. There's nothing I can say that will make a difference."

"Do they have kids?" she asked as they walked out of the waiting room.

He didn't respond right away, but then nodded. "Last I knew they had two."

"Is he your older brother?"

"Yes, he's three years older than me."

Laurel slipped her hand into his. "Are you okay?"

"I will be," Matt said without looking at her.

It wasn't until they were back in his truck that his gaze

met hers. His expression was hard as he said, "And that is why I never want children."

Laurel worked hard to keep her face expressionless. "What do you mean?"

"Our father beat our mother and us boys. Now Steven has started in on his wife. If it's not stopped I have no doubt he'll move on to his kids next. If he hasn't already. I refuse to put myself in that position."

"But you married me. Why would you marry me if you were afraid of becoming like your father?"

Matt gripped the steering wheel with both hands and stared out the front window. "Because I love you. And I was selfish. I wanted you in my life. Thankfully, while we've been together, there have been few instances that have provoked my anger like tonight did."

Laurel sat back against her seat, her stomach churning. "And you didn't think you could be that way with children?"

"I won't take the chance," Matt said as he started the engine. "It was bad enough I took that chance with you."

Laurel turned away as he drove the truck from the parking lot to the street. She stared out the window where the rain left streaks on the glass. The despair she'd been holding at bay flooded her, and it was all she could do not to cry.

The rest of the trip home was made in silence, and very little else was said before they crawled into bed later. Matt seemed to fall asleep quickly, leaving Laurel alone, once again, with her heartache and uncertainty. Whatever hope she'd allowed to grow in the past couple of days was long gone now. There was no indication God was preparing Matt's heart for what she had to tell him. In fact, the opposite seemed to be true now. If anything, the events of the evening had solidified his stance on children.

Matt was glad for a clear day when he woke the next morning. After what had happened the night before, he needed to be out working. Anger still swirled through him. Anger at his brother for what he had done. Anger at himself for letting it affect him the way it had. And he hated that Laurel had seen that ugly part of his past. But there was no going back now. He was actually surprised she hadn't pressed for more information. He still wasn't sure if he would have told her everything. Last night was just the tip of the iceberg, but he'd been spared having to decide what to reveal when she didn't ask him anything further.

His supervisor pushed them hard since they had to make up for the missed work of the previous day, and rain was once again forecast for the next day. Matt was glad for the hard work. It allowed him to use physical activity to work out his emotions. Nothing like swinging a hammer to get anger out.

By the time they quit around eight that evening, Matt was exhausted. The skies were still clear, but the boss said he'd be texting in the morning to let them know if there was work for the day or not. It was almost nine when he let himself into the house. His stomach rumbled its appreciation of the smell of food in the air. It wasn't often that she waited to eat with him since he got home late, so he took it as a good sign.

"I'm going to go take a quick shower," he said when he found Laurel in the kitchen. "Give me ten minutes?"

Laurel nodded and gave him a small smile. It was reminiscent of the way she'd been in recent months. He'd hoped they'd moved past that the other night, but now it appeared she had slipped back into her melancholy mood. He wondered if the events of the previous night had played a role in it. *Don't back away.* Devon's words from the retreat echoed in his mind as he got out of the shower and into a pair of sweats and a t-shirt.

The table was set and food waiting when he walked back into the kitchen. He went to Laurel and slipped an arm around her waist, pressing a kiss to the top of her head.

After they sat down at the table, he took her hand to say grace for the meal. As they dished up their plates, he asked, "How was your day?"

"It was good. Kids are getting antsy to be done though. Not too much teaching going on now. It's more like entertaining." She handed him the salad. "How was yours?"

"Busy. Stu was riding us hard to make up for yesterday. We're just lucky the weather held off. We might not be as fortunate tomorrow." Matt took a drink of his water. "You never told me how your visit with Violet went."

"It went good. We didn't get to visit too much as she was with Dean and Addy most the time. Only came here to sleep basically."

"So it's pretty serious between her and the sheriff?"

"It appears to be." Laurel pushed the food around on her plate. "She seems very happy."

"That's good. Are things still on for you all to be there mid-June?"

"I think so. I haven't heard anything about a change in plans. My guess is that at this point, the only person who would change things might be Cami. I haven't spoken to her since we left Collingsworth."

"I talked to Stu and even though it's our busy time, he's agreed to give me some time off. At the very least I'll try to get up on the weekends."

Laurel nodded but didn't say anything. Matt wished he could read her mind. She hadn't pulled away or rebuffed his affection when he'd hugged her earlier, but there was just something distant about her again.

After they were done eating, he helped her clean up and then suggested they watch a movie together. He even chose one that would appeal more to her than him in hopes of cheering her up. After locking the house for the night, they settled into their bed to watch it, but an hour into the movie, she fell asleep. Since the movie didn't really appeal to him anyway, and he was tired too, Matt shut it off and laid down next to her.

His alarm went off at the usual time the next morning. Matt rolled over and picked up his phone. There was already a text waiting from Stu saying there wouldn't be work that day. Matt settled back down against his pillow, thinking he'd go back to sleep, but having gone to sleep fairly early the night before, he wasn't tired. He lay there for about half an hour, but sleep continued to be elusive. Moving slowly so as not to wake Laurel, he slid out of bed and left the bedroom.

In the quiet of the kitchen, he started a pot of coffee. As he waited for it to finish, he leaned a hip against the counter and began to flip through pile of mail. Laurel had already gone through it and organized everything there. She kept their home running efficiently. Bills were always paid on time. Coupons were clipped for grocery shopping. He never wanted for anything. He knew he was a very blessed man and had no idea what he'd done to deserve her. What he'd told her the other night was true. He'd been selfish enough to take a chance with her because he had wanted her in his life that badly. He hoped she wasn't regretting it now.

He was just pouring himself a cup of the fresh brew when he heard strange noises coming from the bedroom. Concerned, he set the cup back down on the counter and moved quickly down the hall to where he'd left Laurel sleeping.

❧ Chapter Five ❧

THE bed was empty, but the door to their bathroom stood open and the light was on. As he stepped closer, he saw Laurel on her knees, leaning over the toilet, heaving. Alarmed he dropped to the floor beside her.

"Laurel?"

Immediately she turned and pressed a hand to her mouth. Eyes wide, she scooted away from him until her back pressed against the edge of the tub. He could see her throat working as if to keep from throwing up again. But then she turned and pulled herself up to lean over the tub. Matt knelt, helpless, afraid to approach her after the way she'd looked at him when he'd first said her name.

Finally she straightened and turned the water on in the tub. She kept her back to him, but he could see her trembling, and it scared him.

"Laurel? Honey? What's wrong? Do you have the flu again?"

The water stopped, but she didn't turn around right away. He saw her shoulders slump as she sank down on the floor again, her knees drawn tight against her. She was pale and, if he wasn't mistaken, there was fear on her face.

"What's wrong?" Matt demanded, his own fear growing by the second.

He thought she might cry, but then she took a deep breath and looked him straight in the eye. "I'm pregnant."

Matt reared back as she said the words he'd hoped to never hear come out of her mouth. "No."

She didn't respond, just sat there, arms wrapped tightly around her legs.

"No, we agreed. No children. You told me you were okay with that." Matt forced the words past the tight muscles of his throat. "We had a deal."

Still she said nothing as she stared at him with her blue eyes, wide and damp with tears.

Swallowing the bile that rose from his stomach, Matt stood and left the bathroom. He needed to think. He needed some time and space to figure out everything, to try to understand.

He grabbed his phone and wallet from the nightstand on his side of the bed. Desperate to get out of the house, he shoved his feet into his runners but didn't tie them. He took the keys from the table by the door and stepped out into the cool, wet morning. As he backed out of the driveway, Matt wasn't sure where he was going; he just needed to be by himself to deal with a betrayal that cut even more deeply than the one handed to him by his mother almost seventeen years earlier.

∽✦∾

Laurel jumped when she heard the front door slam shut. So much for her plans to tell Matt once school was out. Now she had to somehow make it through the next two days before she could escape to Collingsworth. Though she wasn't surprised by Matt's reaction to her announcement, her fractured heart was now completely broken.

Taking a deep breath, Laurel pushed herself up to sit on the edge of the tub. She didn't entirely trust her legs to hold her just yet, but she needed to start getting ready for school soon. She had to put this aside to deal with later. There was nothing she could do about it now. Matt clearly wasn't in the mood to talk, and, even if he hadn't left the house, there wasn't time to had a long discussion before she had to leave for school anyway. All she could do was pray Matt would be in a more agreeable mood when she got home later.

Hoping a shower would help her feel better, Laurel turned the water on and took off her pajamas. Over the next hour she went through the motions of getting ready for school. By the time she stepped out the front door, she felt marginally better. At least she hoped she would be able to keep up a positive front for the duration of the day. And then just one more day to get through, and this school year would be over.

Matt's truck sat in the driveway when she got home from school. After pulling in next to it, Laurel didn't get out of her car right away. All the way home from school she'd been rehearsing what she needed to say to him. And though it killed her to think about doing even more damage, she knew she needed to tell him about Rose too. In for a penny, in for a pound. Could he hate her any more than she likely did already?

Gathering her purse and jacket from the passenger seat, Laurel got out of the car. She darted for the front door to avoid getting drenched in the continuing downpour. Once inside, she set her purse on the table and hung her jacket in the closet. She knew she was dragging her feet. Matt no doubt knew she was home, but so far he hadn't made an appearance.

She closed her eyes briefly to pray for wisdom then walked toward the kitchen. As she turned the corner, she spotted Matt sitting at the breakfast nook where they ate their meals. He still wore what he'd had on that morning. His arms were braced on the table, and his head was bent. Laurel's heart clenched at the sight of him. She wanted to go to him, sit on his lap, wrap her arms around him and have him tell her everything was going to be okay. But she could see that wasn't going to happen.

Moving slowly she walked to the table and took a seat across from him. She clasped her hands together in her lap. "Can we talk?"

Matt glanced up, and Laurel felt as if the air had been ripped from her lungs. He looked like he'd aged ten years since that morning. And there was no hope or love in his eyes, just despair.

"What is there to talk about?" Matt asked. Dragging his hands across the table, he sat back in his chair. He crossed his arms over his chest, and regarded her with a hardening expression. "We had an agreement. I told you I never wanted kids. You agreed."

Laurel felt a wisp of anger thread its way through the sorrow she'd been carrying all day. "I didn't do this on purpose."

Matt tilted his head. "Then how did it happen?"

"From what I understand, the antibiotics I was on counteracted the birth control. And even though I took them regularly, I was throwing up when I had the flu too. There were days that might have been missed."

"Why didn't you say anything? So we could have used alternate protection?"

"I had a lot going on, Matt. My grandmother had just died. My sisters were all gathering in one place for the first time in a decade. Birth control was the last thing on my mind."

Matt glanced away, his jaw tight. "That still doesn't change how I feel about you being pregnant. I don't want children."

"I'm not going to have an abortion." Laurel placed a protective hand on her abdomen. "I'm not going to give this baby up for adoption."

"You are choosing it over our marriage? Over us?" Matt asked, though by the expression on his face, it was apparent he already knew her answer.

"You're forcing me to. I don't want to. I really don't. But for some reason God has blessed us with this baby, and I plan to raise it. I already had to give away one child. I'm not doing it again."

Matt's gaze whipped back to meet hers. "Again?"

Laurel lifted her chin. Like she'd thought, it really couldn't get any worse, so she might as well put it all out there. "Rose is mine."

"Rose? Your sister, Rose?"

"My daughter, Rose."

Matt shook his head. "I don't understand."

"I was fifteen when I got pregnant with her. Gran was determined to not add another blemish on the Collingsworth name, so she sent me and Cami away to a special school for a year and during that time, I had Rose. She brought Rose back to Collingsworth and told people my mom had dropped off yet another baby. Cami and I came back at the end of the school year, and people were none the wiser that she was really mine. As far as anyone in Collingsworth knew, she was just one more of Elizabeth's daughters."

"Why didn't you tell me?" Matt's expression had moved from bewilderment to anger. "You didn't think I had the right to know?"

"I didn't think I would ever have the opportunity to claim her as my own. I had no reason to think Gran would die before Rose became an adult. And the last time I approached Gran about telling Rose who I really was, she wouldn't even talk to me about it. She told me it wasn't going to happen. End of story. That was just before we decided to get married. I didn't think it would ever be an issue. But then Gran died."

"But still...you didn't think you should tell me? Just...because?" Matt asked.

Laurel frowned at him. "Like you've told me everything from your past? I just met a brother last night I never knew you had."

Matt scowled back at her. "That is different. It would never impact us in the way you having a daughter would."

Silence fell between them. As it stretched on, Laurel realized the happy ending she'd hoped for was not to be. Not with Matt. Not right then. Not wanting to break down in tears in front of him, she swallowed hard then said, "Tomorrow is my last day at school. I will head out to Collingsworth tomorrow night."

"You're leaving?" Matt asked, his face expressionless.

"What else should I do? Are we supposed to just continue on for the next seven months and then when the baby's born, what do we do?"

Matt's head dropped. "I don't know. I just..." He reached up to shove a hand through his hair.

"The one thing that stands between us is not something that can be pushed aside or gotten rid of. You don't want the baby, I do. And now Rose needs me too. I don't see a way to come to any sort of compromise."

When Matt didn't say anything more, Laurel got up and left the kitchen. Once in the hallway leading to their bedroom, she pressed a hand to the wall to keep her balance. She had tried to prepare herself for this. But the painful reality was so far beyond what she had thought it might feel like that she could hardly bear it.

In the bedroom she sat on the bed for a few minutes before getting back up and pulling out her suitcase. Slowly she began to transfer her things from the dresser to the bag. She couldn't pack everything, but took what she figured she'd need for a few weeks. Eventually none of these clothes would fit anyway. At some point she'd come back to get the rest of her things, but for now she only packed the essentials.

After packing, Laurel tried to read as a distraction, but nothing could keep her thoughts from the situation she and Matt were in. Finally, worn out, Laurel crawled into bed early. She hadn't eaten supper, but had absolutely no appetite. However, sleep was elusive with her mind and emotions in such turmoil. She tried to pray, but right then she wondered if God was actually listening. She'd prayed, and she knew her sisters had as well, that God would prepare Matt's heart. Instead their marriage had completely fallen apart. Nothing in his heart had changed. Was this really what God wanted for them?

When the door of the bedroom opened, Laurel lay still, trying to keep her breathing even. She could hear Matt moving around his side of the room and assumed he'd come to get his things and would sleep in another room. But the bed shifted as he sat on it, and then she felt him move beneath the covers next to her.

In the darkness, he reached for her. And though her heart was breaking, though he was the one who was hurting her so very much, Laurel moved into his embrace. She loved this man with all of her aching heart. She felt the tears on his cheeks mingle with hers as Matt pressed his face to hers. And she knew this was goodbye.

Their bittersweet coming together left Laurel sobbing. Matt held her, but said nothing. There were no words he could say that could take away the pain. She clung to him, not wanting the night to end. But soon sleep claimed her weary body, and when she woke in the morning, she was alone.

❧ Chapter Six ❧

LAUREL was in the kitchen at Collingsworth the next Monday morning when Lily came in.

"There's a guy here who says he's supposed to meet with Jessa about the renovations."

Laurel frowned as she started the dishwasher. "She never said anything about it. I'll go talk to him while you get her. I think she's in the greenhouse."

She quickly washed and dried her hands before leaving the kitchen. When she spotted the man standing in the foyer, Laurel came to a stop. "Oh boy."

"Hello, Laurel," he said.

"Does Jessa know you're the one doing this renovation?" Laurel asked without returning his greeting. "Because...wow."

"I don't know. Your grandmother's lawyer just told me to show up this morning to speak with Jessa and whoever else was around."

"Well, I always did enjoy a good fireworks show," Laurel replied wryly then motioned with her hand for him to follow her. "Might as well come on in."

They entered the kitchen at the same time Jessa and Lily came in the back door. Like Laurel, Jessa froze in place at the sight of the man. Her gaze went from Laurel to him and then back to Laurel. All Laurel could do was shrug. She had no idea what was going on.

"Lance," Jessa said, her tone as frigid as the arctic blasts they got in winter. "What are you doing here?"

"Your grandmother hired my company to do the renovations."

She crossed her arms and lifted an eyebrow. "Really? I find that hard to believe."

"What can I say?" Lance shrugged. "She made me an offer I couldn't refuse."

"Why would she do that?" Jessa asked. "Last time I saw you, she told you to get off the property and never come back."

"Guess maybe she reconsidered things in her old age." Lance shifted from one foot to the other, his hands braced on his hips. He was tall, taller than Jessa by a couple of inches at least. He'd once been more like a bean pole, but the man had definitely filled out over the years.

"Huh," Jessa said, the word dripping with doubt.

"Maybe she thought we belonged together after all," Lance said. He grinned then, the movement bringing out his dimples and deepening the lines by his eyes. Laurel almost laughed out loud when he winked at Jessa.

It was kind of nice to have something to focus on besides her own hurting heart. And Lance and Jessa working together guaranteed things would be interesting. Violet had mentioned in passing back during the time she'd been there for the funeral that she thought Jessa had never gotten over Lance. And if the dark hair, dark eyed man had been cute as a teenager, he was downright handsome now that he'd filled out and become more comfortable in his own skin. Laurel figured her sister was going to have her hands full with more than just the renovations.

"Is there some place where we can talk things over?" Lance asked. "I have the plans out in the truck."

"We can do it right here," Jessa said as she motioned to the table in the breakfast nook. "I'm not the only one involved with this."

Lance nodded. "Yes, I know about the clause in the will. But your grandmother figured you'd have the most say since this is essentially your home. Although she did have some pretty clear ideas for how she wanted things done."

"Well, go get your stuff, and we'll see what she's done now."

Lance tipped his head then headed out of the kitchen. When Laurel heard the front door close, she turned to Jessa. "Are you going to be able to handle this?"

Jessa shrugged. "Do I have a choice?"

"What's going on?" Violet asked as she walked into the kitchen. "I thought I heard a man's voice."

"You did," Laurel told her.

"Is Matt here?" she asked hopefully.

Laurel tried to ignore the jump in her heartbeat at the sound of his name and shook her head. "The guy from the renovation company is here to talk with Jessa."

"Ah. I wondered when we'd be meeting him."

Laurel glanced at Jessa. Her older sister just wrinkled her nose and turned her back to them. Violet gave Laurel a "what gives" look. "It's Lance."

Violet's mouth gaped. "Seriously? Lance Evanston? *The* Lance?"

"None other," Laurel assured her.

The front door opened again, and Violet turned as Lance walked back into the kitchen.

"Hi Violet," he said when he spotted her and gave her a wide smile. "Back in town for a while?"

"Permanently, it seems," Violet told him. "Nice to see you again."

Lance quirked an eyebrow. "Permanently? Jessa used to tell me how anxious you were to get away from Collingsworth."

"She was right, but it's funny how falling in love can change one's perspective."

"Very true," Lance said with a nod. He lifted the roll of papers he held in his hand. "Anyone want to go over these plans your grandmother had me draw up?"

Laurel didn't really care what plans were in place. She was there to help where she could to fulfill the terms of the will. It was now more important than ever. If she was going to have to raise two children on her own, the money from the inheritance would be a necessity.

As Violet and Jessa sat down at the table with Lance, Laurel returned to the kitchen and her preparations for dinner. Their conversation floated around her as she worked. Since leaving her home Friday night nothing had held her interest for very long. She felt a bit like she was in a boat on a slow flowing stream without oars or direction, being moved along whether she liked it or not.

The only highlight of this trip home was seeing Rose again. She hadn't told her the news yet about being her mom. Part of her had wanted to blurt it out right away, but Laurel knew that emotionally she wasn't in a good place to deal with all that just yet. She hadn't heard from Matt since she'd left, and she had no idea what would happen next. Would he file for divorce? Was he going to wait for her to do it? If he was, he'd be waiting an awful long time.

As she prayed and cried herself to sleep the last three nights, Laurel had come to realize that no matter how bleak things seemed right then, she would not end her marriage. She wasn't going to go after Matt or try to force him to reconsider, but she wasn't going to be the one to end it either.

"Wow, I'm surprised Gran agreed to basically gutting the

place," Violet said, her voice breaking into Laurel's thoughts.

"Yes, I was too," Lance admitted. "After I got over the shock that she was actually approaching me to do this, I was shocked again at the extent she wanted to renovate."

"Are we going to have to move out?" Jessa asked.

"Not right away. Your grandmother said you guys don't really use the upper west wing."

"No, we don't," Jessa agreed. "The rooms we use are all on the east side. Gran was the only one with a room on the west side."

"So we'll start there and do those rooms first. Then once we're done, maybe you could move into those and we can do the other ones. There isn't too much down here she wanted changed aside from completely updating the kitchen and replacing all the windows and other damage we might find. Maybe refinishing the wood floors if you decided you wanted that done."

"Did she tell you why she was doing this?" Violet asked.

Curiosity roused, Laurel wiped her hands and went to stand behind Violet's chair to look at the plans now spread out on the table.

Lance sighed. "I asked her, but she didn't give a straightforward answer. She just said something about wanting to give you girls a fresh start and the ability to make this place your own."

"But if she wanted us to make the place our own, why did she lay out all these plans without consulting us?" Jessa asked. "How much say do we actually have in what's going to happen?"

"Not much in the actual layout of things. I worked these plans up for her, taking into account the things she said she wanted. Like a bathroom for each room. Reworking them now would be time consuming and depending what you want, maybe not even possible." He gestured to the plans on the table. "Was there something in particular you were wondering about changing?"

Laurel looked over at Jessa. This was her home more than any of theirs, so it was only natural Jessa would be the one with ideas. Her older sister stared at the plans for a minute before shaking her head.

"No, I guess not. But can we choose things like paint color and the type of flooring?"

Lance nodded. "Yes, that's not a problem. She said to leave anything that didn't affect the actual floor plan of the house to your discretion."

"This is just nuts," Jessa said with a shake of her head.

Lance laughed. "I think it's going to be fun." He looked up at Laurel. "Your grandmother said your husband is in construction and might be able to help some."

Laurel felt Jessa and Violet's gazes on her. She swallowed hard. "It's a busy time for their business. I doubt he'll be able to get away."

"That's too bad," Lance said. "Hopefully I'll get to meet him at some point. Your grandmother seemed to really like him."

"Really?" Laurel asked. "She never said anything like that to me."

"She did like him," Jessa said. "She was like that, you know."

"Like what?" Violet asked.

"She rarely would praise or appreciate someone to their face, but in talking with others she would." Jessa turned to Violet. "When you talked to her, did she ever say she was proud of what you were doing?"

"Nope. Never," Violet said with a shake of her head.

"Yet she told me repeatedly she was," Jessa informed her.

"When we talked she'd always tell me all about you guys and how you were doing such great things," Violet said.

"Exactly," Jessa replied. "Anyway, to get back on track with this—can you bring us paint and flooring samples at some point?"

Lance nodded. "Actually, the sooner, the better. We will need to place orders for some of the stuff most likely. Are we still on track to start in a couple of weeks?"

"As far as I know," Jessa said. "We hadn't heard from Cami, but she said she'd be back by the fifteenth."

"Okay, good," Lance said as he began to roll up the plans. "One other thing, you may want to look into renting one of those portable storage bins. It would be convenient to move things into, if need be."

Laurel went back to the sink to finish cleaning and peeling the carrots for the roast. Violet and Jessa walked Lance out and were deep in discussions about the plans when they returned. As she worked she found her mind drifting to Matt. It was a sunny day which meant he was at work. She wondered if he'd been eating. For the most part, she had done all the cooking. He would make the odd breakfast and had been in charge of all grill-related meals, but left to his own devices, he usually resorted to canned goods or takeout.

She missed taking care of him. He had taken care of her too. After their wedding, they'd easily fallen into the roles that suited them best in their relationship. And she missed that. She knew people said you shouldn't look to someone to complete you, that you should already be a confident, whole person on your own. But right then, she felt like she was missing an important part of herself. The part of her that was so intertwined with Matt. Would she ever feel whole again?

"Hey!"

Laurel jumped and turned to see her sisters staring at her. "Sorry. Were you talking to me?"

"We were trying to," Violet said. "You okay?"

Laurel shrugged. "What did you want?"

"Just wondering if you needed help," Jessa said. "I don't want you to overdo it."

"I'm fine," she assured them. "I found it exhausting when I had to work all day, but doing a little bit of cooking and stuff here is not wearing me out at all."

"Well, be sure and let us know if you need us to do anything." Violet came to stand beside her. "So what's for supper?"

Laurel gave her a small smile. "Liver and onions."

"Ewww," Violet said, wrinkling her nose. "Uh, I think Dean said something about taking me out."

Laurel shook her head. "You're so gullible!"

"So we're not having...what you said?"

"I can't eat that myself. There's no way I would make others eat it." Laurel held up a carrot. "We're having a roast."

"Oh, much better." Violet gave her a quick hug. "I'm so glad you like to cook."

"Me, too," Jessa piped up. "Though if I start to gain weight I may change my mind."

"I'm glad to do it for you," Laurel said. "And I'm making plenty, so if you'd like to invite Dean and Addy, there would be enough."

"Really?" Violet glanced at Jessa. "Is that okay with you?"

"Fine by me. The more the merrier. Unless it's Lance," Jessa said with a frown. "I can't believe Gran hired him."

"That woman continues to manipulate things from the grave," Violet remarked drily. "Every day I wake up wondering if this will be the day when something new develops from plans Gran put in place before she died."

Laurel fought to keep her attention on what her sisters were saying. She found it harder and harder to stay plugged into what was going on around her as the drifting feeling swept her up again. Her anchor was gone.

Eventually Jessa and Violet headed back to what they'd been doing before Lance had shown up, leaving Laurel alone with her thoughts. Which wasn't necessarily a good thing.

❧ *Chapter Seven* ❧

MATT pulled his truck to a stop along the curb in front of the house that matched the address he'd managed to find for his brother's house. It wasn't in the nicest part of town, but it didn't look like a bad place to raise a family. He stepped out of the truck and made his way to the door, enjoying the scent of freshly cut grass on the evening air.

"How are you doing, Melly?" Matt asked when his sister-in-law answered his knock.

Melly glanced over her shoulder, apprehension on her face. "I'm fine. You need to go."

"What's wrong?" Matt looked past her but couldn't see anything in the room beyond her. The curtains were drawn leaving the room shadowed. "Is Steven here?"

Another furtive glance, then she shook her head.

Matt sighed, more than convinced that his brother lurked in the house somewhere. "He's not supposed to be here, is he? If he shows up, you need to call the police."

"You'd like that, wouldn't you, brother?" Steven stepped from the shadows to stand behind his wife. He laid his hand on her shoulder and forcibly moved her out of his way.

"You're the one who needs to leave. Don't think I won't lay a world of hurt on you."

"You're just making things worse for yourself," Matt said with a shake of his head. He looked back at Melly. "Is this really the life you want?"

"And if it's not?" Steven didn't allow his wife to respond. "You gonna kill me?"

Swallowing back the anger that swelled in him, Matt said, "Tempting, but no."

"Then I suggest you leave." Steven reached out and shoved Matt. As Matt stepped back, his brother stormed past him, yelling obscenities.

Turning back to Melly, Matt pulled a card he'd printed out earlier and handed it to her. "If you need anything, give me a call. Please."

She took the card and slid it into the pocket of her jeans, but remained silent.

Knowing there was nothing more he could do, Matt spun around to see what his brother was up to. He saw Steven heading for his truck.

"You put one mark on my truck and you can add vandalism to your rap sheet," Matt called out. Like most men, his vehicle was an extension of himself and there was no way he'd stand by and let his brother damage it.

Apparently the threat in his voice was enough to deter Steven from his intent. He shouted a few more choice words at Matt and then veered toward the side of the house. Matt wasted no time getting back in his truck and leaving. He didn't go too far. Just a block away, he pulled over and took the time to call the police to let them know that Steven was at the house with Melly. He didn't know if the cops would show up or not, but at least there would be a record of him having been at the house.

Walking into the kitchen forty-five minutes later, Matt set the bag of takeout he'd stopped for on the table. She'd been gone three days, and it wasn't getting any easier. Though he had once assumed he'd spend the rest of his life alone, now faced with that reality after having experienced life with Laurel, Matt found it impossible to consider.

He took the food out of the bag and put a couple of the containers right into the fridge. They would be for his supper the next night. After dumping a container onto a plate and sticking it into the microwave to heat up, Matt took his dinner, such as it was, into the living room and sat down on the couch in front of the television.

And ate his supper. Alone.

The dirty plate joined the others in the sink in the kitchen twenty minutes later. He went to the guest bathroom to take a shower and snagged a clean t-shirt and sweats from a pile of clothes. When he'd come home Friday night to find Laurel gone, he'd pulled all his clothes out of his chest of drawers and dumped them on the bed in the guest room. He had yet to step foot back in the room he'd shared with her. Every night so far he'd slept on the couch in the living room with the television on.

He didn't sleep that well, but Matt figured it wouldn't matter where he slept. The first night he'd laid down on the couch with the television off, but instead of sleep, thoughts tumbled through his mind. Confusing, conflicting thoughts. Since that night, he'd put the television on and watched it until his numbed mind shut down.

He wanted to phone Laurel, to hear her voice. But so far, he'd resisted. Nothing had changed on his end, and he assumed the same for her since she hadn't contacted him either. They were at an impasse. A heartbreaking standoff.

And while Laurel had the comfort of her sisters and the presence of her daughter and the baby she carried, he was alone. It was how he had planned to live until Laurel had slipped into his life three years ago. Her gentle demeanor and shy smile had reeled him in. While other women had been more obvious in their desire for his attention, it had been her quiet friendship that had finally made the walls around his heart crumble. She'd told him later, she hadn't even set out to be anything more than friends. And yet somehow they'd found the perfect match in each other, until Thursday morning when their paths had diverged like an axe splitting a piece of wood.

On his way back to the living room, he passed the shelves that held pictures of the two of them Laurel had put there over the past two years. He reached past more recent ones to snag the frame that held the image of the two of them on their wedding day. It hadn't technically been an elopement because Laurel had planned it in great detail, but it had been very, very small. The only ones present had been the pastor and his wife and a handful of friends who had joined them on the shores of the lake that Friday evening in August almost three years ago. She had been so beautiful in her simple, yet elegant white dress. Even though it had been small, Matt had encouraged her to get the dress of her dreams.

He traced a finger over Laurel's image. How could he make this right? He just couldn't get past the memory of being a child and suffering at his father's hands. The same man who would toss a ball with them and tell them he loved them, would lose his temper over the slightest thing and then it was pain and fear for Matt and Steven. And one night Matt's own anger had overwhelmed him. Fear for his life had been the spark, but anger had been the gasoline that had sent him over the edge. And at the tender age of ten he'd learned just how deadly his anger could be.

Even though his mother and brother hadn't supported his story, the cops had taken one look at his broken, bruised body and believed him when he said he'd killed his father out of self-defense. His mother had tried to place all the blame on him, but it was hard for her to explain away the bruises she herself bore. He had never understood why the two people who had suffered alongside him at the hand of his father had betrayed him. As the police took him away that horrible night, he'd look over his shoulder at his mother one last time, longing for her to come to him. That was the last time he'd seen her.

He'd been in and out of foster homes over the next eight

years. People would only take him on a temporary basis given his history. Not that he blamed them. Even he never knew if something was going to set him off. Then he'd met Devon Sinclair in his senior year of high school. The star football player had befriended him, and soon he was spending as much time as he could with the Sinclair family. They'd welcomed him and opened their home without hesitation. Though he hadn't told Devon too much about his past when they were younger, Matt had thought it was only fair that his parents know his past so they could decide whether they wanted him as a friend for their son.

They had listened, and offered no judgment, only love. And from them he learned about forgiveness through Jesus and the unconditional love of God. But none of what they'd shared with him, none of what he'd come to believe could ever convince him that having children of his own was a good idea. And he'd rather lose the woman he loved than take a chance that in a split second, he could do to his child, what his father had done to him.

He set the wedding portrait down on the shelf with the other pictures. Now he would continue on with the life he had originally envisioned for himself. The one where he was alone, but at least safe in the knowledge he would never hurt someone he loved.

∽✦∾

Laurel stared out at the darkness beyond her window. Yet another day had passed with no word from Matt. They had never gone this long without talking since they day he'd asked her out on their first date. The gaping hole in her life and heart seemed unfathomable and endless.

There was a light rap on her door. Laurel brushed her fingers over her cheeks to make sure no tears had escaped.

"Come in," she called out. The door opened, and Violet poked her head in.

"Up for a chat?" she asked.

Laurel wasn't really, but she nodded. She gestured to the

bed as she walked toward it. Violet joined her there, crossing her legs as she settled on the bed.

"Are you doing okay?" Violet asked, but then held out her hand. "Wait. Don't answer that."

"Uh...okay," Laurel said, a bit confused by her sister's response.

"I've been reading a book on relationships and one of the things it said was to ask questions that encouraged conversation. So, let me rephrase my original question." Violet leaned toward her slightly, concern evident in her eyes. "Is there anything I can do to help you through this?"

Laurel sat for a moment then said, "Actually, yes. Can you talk to me about something besides this mess with Matt? I'm dwelling on it too much. I could use a distraction."

Violet straightened, a sudden gleam in her eye. "Really? Because there is something I'd love to talk to you about."

Curious, Laurel nodded.

"Okay," Violet said and with a glance at the closed door, she scooted closer to Laurel. "I heard again from Tom, my detective guy, and he said he had more news on Mama."

"Really? Did he find her?" Laurel still wasn't sure how she felt about Violet trying to locate their mother, but if this would give her something else to focus on, she was going to take advantage of it.

"No, he didn't find her, but he came across a nurse who remembered hearing about Mama in a hospital in Deluth."

"After she delivered one of us?"

Violet shook her head. "No. The timeframe the woman gave would have placed it right after Mama dropped off Lily."

"What did she say about her?"

"The woman was rather reluctant to disclose information, but I guess Tom can be persuasive. Anyway, she said that the rumor was that Julia Collingsworth's daughter had been brought in after being beaten. That was all the woman heard, and Tom could find no record of Mama being in the hospital or of her dying. However, he's still not convinced she's alive, especially in light of the nurse's recollection of how severe her injuries were. At least, according to the rumor mill in the hospital."

"That's horrible though," Laurel said, her thoughts going back to the night in the hospital with Matt and his brother. Why did people beat up others? It was something she couldn't begin to comprehend. "Who would have done that to her?"

"My first thought is the guy who was with her." Violet shrugged. "But who really knows. It seems Gran managed to cover up that trail as well. I mean, Duluth? What would Mama have been doing there?"

Given what Laurel knew about their mom, Duluth made just about as much sense as anywhere else. "So Tom is still looking for more information on that?"

"Yes, but so far everything has led to a dead end."

"While I'm glad Gran had money, I'm thinking that it made it way too easy for her to pay people off and hide things."

Violet nodded. "That Collingsworth money is definitely a double edged sword when it comes to stuff like this."

When her phone chirped, Violet glanced at the display and smiled. "It's Dean. I'll talk to you later." She pressed a kiss to Laurel's cheek and then answered the phone as she slid walked toward the door.

Alone in the room, Laurel got off the bed and went through her night time ritual. She was thankful to Violet for giving her something to think about other than her miserable situation. Before Violet had told her about her search when she'd come to visit, it had been ages since she'd given her mom any thought. Now though, she did wonder where Mama might have ended up after dropping off Lily.

Unfortunately, her mom could only occupy her thoughts for so long, and her last thoughts brought hot tears to her eyes as the ache from missing Matt intensified. And, as she had done every night since arriving at Collingsworth, Laurel cried herself to sleep.

Around two in the morning, Laurel found herself awake and unable to fall back asleep. Not wanting to continue tossing and turning, she climbed out of bed and left her room. The rest of the house was quiet and dark, but she had no problem finding her way downstairs. Many years of sneaking through the house at night had made her very familiar with every squeaky floorboard and light switch.

She went to the kitchen first and got a glass of milk, then made her way to the library. As a teen she'd spent a lot of time in that room. Gran had kept a tight rein on their social lives, so she'd escaped into books a lot. Although, she had found time to get pregnant.

Laurel walked to the bookcases that lined one wall. As she drank her milk, she ran a finger along the spines of the books, reading the titles. She came to one that was upside down, so she set her glass down and pulled the book out to put it back in properly. As she pulled it out, a packet fell to the floor. Laurel looked at the book in her hand, surprised to see the inside of it had been completely cut out, leaving room for the packet.

She shoved the empty book back into its place on the shelf—correct side up—and bent to pick up the packet. Scrawled on the front in Gran's familiar handwriting were the words "My Girls". Laurel turned it over and saw the envelope was sealed. She wondered if she should wait until the others were there to open it.

Her thoughts went back to the conversation she'd had earlier with Violet. Would this packet have answers to the questions Violet had been looking for? There was no way she could wait until morning to see what was inside of it. She settled into the winged chair near the bookcase and after a moment's hesitation, ran her finger under the flap to unseal the envelope.

Laurel slid the papers out onto her lap. She knew part of the reason she was so eager to read the contents was to take her mind off everything else going on. And she was pretty sure Violet wouldn't get too upset with her for not waiting.

However, she would wait to tell Jessa until she'd talked with Violet, regardless of the contents.

She picked up the top sheet and unfolded it. The date at the top of the page was four months earlier, not that long before Gran's death. The older woman must have had a good idea of what was to come.

My darling girls,

I'm going to take a wild guess and say it's probably Laurel who has found this. Given your love for the library and the books there, as well as your need for things to be orderly, I'm sure you couldn't resist fixing the book I've hidden this in.

I don't know how to tell you all this other than to just say it. In addition to the five of you, your mother also gave birth to a son. He is three years older than Lily. Unfortunately, I did not feel equipped to raise a boy. I'm sure some of you feel I was ill-equipped to raise any of you, but that's beside the point. I wanted the boy to have a good male role model, and there was none to be had here at Collingsworth Manor. To that end, I gave him to some good people to raise. He knows who he is, and I have seen him a few times over the years.

It just so happened that around the time your mother brought him to me, Jonathan and Sylvia's son was visiting from California. They had been unable to have children (though that changed in the years that followed) and they were thrilled to have a chance to raise a child. There was no formal adoption. I named him before they took him with the understanding he would always know who he was and that one day he would meet the rest of his family.

The papers contained here will give you an idea of who he is and what he's been doing. Also, he will not be mentioned in the will, but he is provided for in the same way you girls have been. Should you not have found this before the six month mark following my death, Stan has been instructed to tell you about it. Where you go from here is up to the six of you. I pray you will come together as siblings, but I realize that may take time, if it happens at all.

I did what I thought was right at the time. William has grown into a wonderful man, and I hope you will accept him as your brother.

I know that I have left you with many questions and precious few answers. I have always done what I thought was best for you and our family. There are some secrets I hope never see the light of day, but I have a feeling that in time, all will be revealed. I just hope at that time you will try to understand why I did what I did. Every decision I made was out of love for you and the desire to protect each of you and our family. Please always remember that. I love each of you with all my heart and, while some of you may feel differently, please be assured that it is true. I might not know how to express it well, but you girls are my world and each of you is very important to me. Always remember that.

Much love,

Gran

✌ Chapter Eight ✆

LAUREL read the letter through twice. Given that Violet had basically said as much about another child, it didn't come as a complete shock. She set the letter aside and picked up the other papers. The first thing she saw was a picture. As she stared at it, Laurel was able to see the similarities between William and the rest of them. He was definitely a Collingsworth, and probably the luckiest of them having been raised away from the town named for their family and a grandmother who had been hard to live with.

Before she looked any further, Laurel scooped it all up and left the library. She quickly climbed the stairs and went to Violet's door. It was closed, but she didn't knock, just opened it and walked through the darkness to her sister's bed.

"Hey, Vi! Wake up!" Laurel put her hand on the mattress and pressed on it several times.

"What the..." Violet rolled over. "Laurel? What on earth? Is something wrong?"

Laurel found the switch for the bedside lamp and

switched it on.

"Good grief, Laurel!" Violet covered her eyes with her arm. "What is your problem?"

She climbed onto the bed beside her sister and said, "You were right!"

"Of course I was. Wait. What?" Violet lowered her arm. "What was I right about?"

"We have a brother!"

Violet's brows drew together as she looked over at the clock on her bedside table. "And you figured this out at...two o'clock in the morning? What on earth, Laurel?" She flopped back on her pillows, pulled her blanket up and closed her eyes.

"No, seriously, Vi. I couldn't sleep so I went down to the library and while I was looking at the books, I found something from Gran."

Violet opened one eye. "From Gran?" Then the other. "About a brother?"

Laurel nodded. She looked through the papers in her lap and pulled out the picture. "Meet William Collingsworth."

Violet pushed herself up to a sitting position and reached for the photo. She stared down at it for a minute then looked back up at Laurel. "Am I dreaming?"

"Nope. No dream."

"Oh, wow!" Violet looked again at the picture.

"Gran included a letter and some other stuff about him. He's been living with Roger and Deanna Miller's family in California, but he knows all about us." Laurel handed her the letter Gran had written. As Violet read through it, Laurel went through the other papers. It looked like his guardians had kept Gran up to date on his life, sending report cards and copies of other achievement awards. It seemed he wasn't just smart, but athletic and passionate about his faith too.

"This is unbelievable," Violet said. "When we talked about it at your place, I certainly didn't anticipate confirmation so quickly."

"I know, right?" Laurel handed her some more of the papers. "So weird to think there's another one of us out there."

"Sometimes I have to wonder about Mama. I mean, had she never heard of birth control?" Violet sifted through the papers. "Not that I'd wish any of us away."

Laurel laughed. "Oh, I think we've all wished each other away at varying times over the years."

Violet grinned. "Yes. This is true."

"What are you two doing?" Laurel straightened and felt Violet do the same. Jessa stood in the open doorway. "It's like three in the morning. Why are you two up and making noise?"

"Oh, sorry," Violet said. "I didn't realize you could hear us."

"I got up to go to the bathroom and then thought I heard someone moving around."

"That was probably me," Laurel confessed. "Sorry."

Jessa ventured into the room. "What's all this?"

Laurel glanced at Violet. Her sister just shrugged. They had to tell Jessa about this sooner or later, so Laurel recapped her earlier conversation with Violet and then how she came across the packet in the library. She handed the photo to Jessa. "Gran said he's three years older than Lily."

Jessa's brow furrowed as she sank down on the bed. "I know him."

"You do?" Violet said, surprise in her voice.

Jessa nodded. "He came for Jonathan's funeral. I think it was about five years ago. I just met him in passing. I don't even remember his name."

"It's William," Laurel said, then as something occurred to her, she continued, "Was he here for Gran's funeral?"

"I don't remember him," Violet said with a shrug. "But then, I wasn't really too focused on who all was present at the memorial service."

"Me either," Jessa added.

"So what do we do now?" Laurel asked.

Violet handed the rest of the papers to Jessa. "I guess maybe we should talk to Stan. He seems to be the keeper of Gran's secrets. It sounded like he was supposed to tell us about William if we didn't find out on our own. Wonder how many other secrets he's holding onto, waiting for us to discover them."

Jessa shuffled the papers together and slid them into the envelope when Laurel handed it to her. "I'll give Stan a call in the morning. What exactly do we want though?"

"I'd like to meet him," Violet said immediately. "If he has any interest in us, I'd like to get to know him."

"Me, too," Laurel agreed. "I think it would be great if he could come here for a bit."

"So when I talk to Stan, I'll tell him we're interested in meeting him if he's willing."

"Yes." Laurel looked more closely at Jessa. "Are you okay with this?"

Jessa looked up and gave her a weak smile. "To be honest, I'm not sure what to think. I can't believe Gran kept something like this from me. I mean, I thought we were close enough she'd tell me about stuff, but guess I was wrong."

Laurel leaned over and slipped her arm around Jessa's

shoulders. "I'm sure she only kept things like this from you to protect the family. I don't understand that need myself. It was like she had a mandate to never let the world see the cracks in the family. I'm actually surprised she didn't farm all of us out, in order to keep Mama's lifestyle from being revealed."

"I know she was fanatical about protecting the Collingsworth name. I didn't understand it, but she never let anyone, even me, see weakness in her." Jessa's voice trembled as she said, "I really miss her. But then after finding out stuff like this, I get really angry. We had a sibling we could have known all these years but for whatever reason, she sent him off to live with strangers."

"I gave up trying to understand why she did what she did a long time ago," Violet said with a sigh. "All I know is that it had to be very stressful living a life so filled with secrets and the walls she used to keep people at a distance."

Jessa drew her legs up and wrapped her arms around them. "I know I'm like Gran in a lot of ways, but I certainly hope I don't ever feel so compelled to hide things in my life."

"Not to worry, Jess," Violet said, "we'll make sure you keep it honest."

Laurel laughed along with the other two, grateful for a reprieve from the darkness that had been hanging over her for the past several days. She was a little bummed when Violet yawned, and Jessa slid off the bed.

"Well, I don't know about you two, but I need to get a bit more sleep," Jessa said. "We can discuss this more tomorrow after I talk with Stan."

After Jessa left, Laurel was a little slow to leave. She wasn't too excited about returning to her empty bed.

"Hey, you want to sleep here with me?" Violet asked as if she had read Laurel's mind.

"Do you mind?" Laurel didn't want to inconvenience her.

"Not at all. But don't get upset if I kick you in the night." Violet smiled and lifted an eyebrow. "I suppose I need to get used to sharing my bed eventually."

Laurel slid under the covers and turned on her side to face Violet. "Do you think Dean is going to propose soon?"

Violet glanced over her shoulder at Laurel before snapping out the light. "Your guess is as good as mine."

Though she wished it were Matt in the bed with her, Laurel was glad for the company as the room settled into darkness. "Night, Vi."

"Night, sis."

Laurel lay in silence for about a minute before asking, "Do you think Jessa is really okay with all this? I mean, none of the rest of us were as close to Gran as she was. I wonder if she thought maybe Gran would tell her about stuff like this, even if she didn't tell the rest of us."

When Violet didn't respond right away, Laurel thought maybe she'd fallen asleep already. But then Violet said, "I'm sure it bothers her, but just like her grieving, I'm sure she'll deal with it alone in private. I've only seen her break down once or twice since Gran's death, and yet I'm sure it has upset her more than that."

"I worry about her," Laurel confessed. "Especially since Lance is back in the picture. I know that can't be easy for her. Really wonder about Gran on that one."

"Yes, I know. Especially now that I know a little more about her past, I can't figure out why she would have come between Jessa and Lance in the first place."

"No doubt another secret." Laurel turned onto her back. "Sorry, didn't mean to keep you awake. Just kinda glad to have something to focus on besides my mess of a life."

"I understand. I wish you didn't have to deal with all of that. I feel guilty being happy with Dean when you're struggling and who knows how Jessa is feeling."

"Don't worry about being happy. I'm so glad for you. Just make sure you know everything about Dean ahead of time, so you don't have any nasty surprises in the long run."

"Secrets have already gotten us in trouble. Almost derailed us before we got started. Thankfully God worked it out for us."

"I sure hope He's going to somehow work it out for Matt and me," Laurel said even though she really didn't feel a lot of hope right then.

"I hope so too," Violet replied. "We'll just keep praying for His will to prevail."

This time when the room fell into silence, Laurel didn't say anything more. Not wanting to get dragged down, she focused her thoughts instead on what they'd learned about their new brother. Finally she drifted off to sleep. When she woke in the morning, it was to a rolling stomach and an empty bed.

A little while later, when she was finally feeling more alert, Laurel made her way downstairs. She found Jessa and Violet in the kitchen talking.

"Did you get hold of Stan?" she asked as she joined them.

"He's going to come by in about an hour," Jessa said. "I'm going to press him for any other secrets he might be holding for Gran. This is getting a little ridiculous."

Violet nodded. "I would really like to find out what happened to Mama."

Laurel glanced between her two sisters, wincing at the frown on Jessa's face.

"That's not exactly high on my list of things to know," Jessa said. "If she couldn't be bothered to stay in contact with us, so be it."

"It's possible she hasn't been able to," Violet said. "But regardless, I'm going to ask Stan about her again. Just so you know."

Laurel thought Jessa might object but she just shrugged and said, "I understand why you'd want to know. You knew her more than I ever did."

Pressing a hand to her stomach, Laurel went to make herself some tea and toast. At least they weren't fighting about it. Maybe they had all mellowed with age. Though Jessa could still take a hard line on certain things, she seemed to have softened in some ways. Hopefully it stayed that way through the next couple of months which were sure to be trying at best, especially once Cami came home.

Stan arrived a little after eleven. They didn't waste much time over small talk. After they all sat down at the table, Jessa handed him the packet of papers and said, "Can you tell us more about this?"

He took the packet and slid the papers out onto the table. It didn't take him long to look through them. "Yes, your grandmother gave me permission to give you any more information on William once you found this. Or, if you hadn't found it six months after her death, I was to tell you about him."

"Does William know Gran died?" Violet asked.

Stan nodded. "They were actually here for the funeral, but they understood it wasn't the best time to reveal William's existence."

"That's probably true," Jessa agreed. "Will you contact them now that we know?"

"Yes. It was your grandmother's wish that you all meet, provided you were willing to do that."

"I am," Violet responded right away.

Jessa was a little slower. "Yes, I think we are willing."

When Stan glanced at her, Laurel nodded as well.

"And what about Cami? Should we wait to hear from her?"

Jessa laughed. "I doubt she'd care one way or the other. We haven't been able to get in touch with her, so it's her loss."

"As long as all three of you are in agreement," Stan said.

"We are," Violet assured him. "It seems odd that we have a sibling out there that we haven't met."

"There is just the one, right?" Laurel asked.

"As far as I know," Stan replied. "I do have one other thing to give you though." He lifted his briefcase onto the table and snapped it open so he could pull out a file folder. After setting it on the floor again, Stan opened the file. "Your grandmother didn't know for sure if this information was accurate, but she wanted me to give it to you if you wanted it, and then you could figure it out for yourselves." He handed Jessa several papers that were stapled together. "At some point, perhaps when your mother dropped each of you off, Julia recorded what Elizabeth would tell her about your fathers."

"You have information on our fathers?" Violet asked.

"Yes. Those papers are what Julia gave me."

Jessa passed the papers to Violet without even looking at them. "I already know who my father is."

Violet paused as she reached for the papers. "You do?"

"Yes, I found out a few years ago."

"Wow. You never said." Violet took the papers and looked down at them.

Jessa shrugged. "It didn't seem that important."

Laurel wondered if Jessa really didn't care about these unknown parts of their past, or if it was just her way of dealing with it all. She certainly was curious.

"My dad's name isn't familiar to me," Violet said. She glanced at Laurel. "But this confirms what I've suspected for you and Cami."

Laurel took the papers and looked for her name. "We have the same dad?"

"It seems that way," Violet said. "Not really surprising though. You and Cami have always looked the most alike."

Maybe their mom had managed to find a few years of happiness with someone, but Laurel wondered what had happened to their dad. Clearly their mother moved on at some point since William's father was listed as someone else, as was Lily's.

"I know I've asked you before, Stan," Violet began, "and I hate to belabor the point, but since we're spilling secrets...do you have any information on our mom?"

Stan shook his head, a sad look on his face. "I really don't. If your grandmother had any legal dealings with regards to Elizabeth, she didn't use me."

Jessa froze in the process of standing, and then sank back down on her chair. "Are you telling me that there might be another lawyer out there who Gran dealt with?"

"It's certainly possible," Stan said. "I always got the feeling she wasn't entirely forthcoming on a few subjects. Your mother being one of them."

"And the other subjects you wondered about?" Violet prompted.

❧ *Chapter Nine* ❧

*L*AUREL held her breath, hoping there would be no more revelations. She was getting really sick of secrets.

"I wondered about another child a few years back, but then she ended up giving me the information on William last year. Those were the two main subjects." Stan gave a slow shake of his head. "I don't really understand a lot of the decisions your grandmother made, but I wasn't paid to question them. I was paid to carry out her wishes."

"But now that she's gone, who do you work for?" Jessa asked.

Laurel wondered if Stan would take offense at Jessa's blunt question, but he didn't appear to.

"I work for your grandmother's estate," Stan said. "But I've already done some things that weren't how she wanted them." He gestured to the papers in front of Laurel. "I was to wait until you asked for those before producing them. But I thought maybe it was time to just get out everything I knew."

"Thank you, Stan," Violet said. "I wish Gran hadn't felt the need for all these secrets, but she must have had her reasons."

"The overwhelming reason I always seemed to get from her was to protect the family name," Stan revealed. "Being the only child and having her family do what was necessary to pass the Collingsworth name on to her, I think Julia felt the weight of responsibility heavily. And when your mother kind of went off the rails, she seemed to be even more desperate to keep more things from reflecting badly on the family."

"Well, I hope we can bring a bit more honesty to the family name," Violet said. "We're not perfect, but I think the Collingsworth legacy can handle a few dings. We're trying our best."

"I think you will do just fine." Stan smiled. "I'd better get back to the office. I'll let you know when I've contacted William and his family."

Laurel stood with the others and thanked Stan before Jessa walked him to the front door. She heard muffled conversation and then the front door closed, but Jessa didn't return to the kitchen. Violet got up and walked toward the back door.

"She's going to the greenhouse," she said.

Laurel joined her and watched as their older sister took the path that led through some trees to her greenhouse. "She's upset."

Violet sighed. "Yes, I think so. Not too surprising though really."

"Should we go to her?" Laurel hated the thought of Jessa being upset and on her own.

"I think we need to give her a little space. If she wanted us around, she'd have come back." Violet turned from the door. "In the meantime, I'm going to call Tom with the information on my father. Did you want me to have him look for yours as well?"

"I don't know," Laurel replied. "I haven't thought about my father in years. Maybe I'll wait and talk to Cami. See what she wants to do."

Violet nodded and went to pick up the paper from the table. "I'll let you know what Tom says."

Left alone in the kitchen, Laurel decided she didn't want to leave Jessa alone. She stepped out onto the large back porch. The day was warm, but a breeze rustled the leaves of the nearby trees. Slowly she walked toward the greenhouse. The smell of earth greeted her as she stepped into the structure.

"Jess?" Laurel called out, not seeing her sister immediately.

Jessa appeared at the end of a row. "What's up?"

Laurel moved toward her, amazed at the number of plants Jessa had growing there. "Are you okay?"

Jessa tugged on a pair of gardening gloves and moved toward a large bench at the back of the green house. "To be honest, I'm not sure. I'm feeling a bit...beat up by everything that keeps coming up."

Laurel went to her side and slipped an arm around her waist. "I'm sorry."

Jessa turned to return the hug. "I suppose right now, of everyone, you're probably the one who understands what I'm feeling the best as these secrets keep being revealed. I just keep wondering what else is going to pop up."

"Are you upset with Gran over this? Or is it something else?"

Jessa moved some pots around and hefted a large bag of soil unto the work bench. "Yeah, I'm mad at her. Did she have to keep so many life changing secrets from me? From us? I mean, a brother? Really? And then asking Lance to do the renovations. What is that about?"

Laurel leaned a hip against the wooden bench. "That one is a bit perplexing, for sure. I thought he got married."

Jessa shrugged. "Me too. It was something Gran and I never talked about after it happened."

"Did you ever forgive her for forcing Lance to leave you?"

She didn't answer as she dumped some soil into a pot. But then Jessa paused, her hands resting on the table. "I don't know. I guess after I heard he'd gone on to get engaged so quickly, I figured she'd been right. Having him show back up now, at Gran's request, is more than a little confusing."

Laurel touched the leaf of an already potted plant. "Would you ever consider something with him again?"

"Nope," Jessa said without hesitation. "That ship had sailed. Plus, we're different people now."

"Never say never," Laurel said.

Jessa shot a glance her way and wrinkled her nose. "Please don't try any matchmaking. Besides, I've been in contact with someone lately that's kind of caught my interest."

Laurel lifted a brow. "Really? Gonna spill the beans?"

"His name is Gareth Williams. He's been teaching at the college." Jessa set aside one pot and reached for another. "He stopped by the shop last week to ask me about my gardening and the greenhouse. Apparently he's quite a gardener himself and practices something called square foot gardening. He's going to stop by sometime to have a look at the setup here and share his experience."

"Sounds interesting. And right up your alley with the gardening thing. Is he from around here?"

"Originally he's from Australia, so he's got that delightful accent," Jessa said with a smile. "We'll see."

Laurel was happy to hear Jessa had something good to focus on in addition to all the stuff they were dealing with from Gran. "Be sure to introduce us when he comes."

Jessa nodded. "As long as you promise to behave."

Laurel pressed a hand to her chest. "Me? Not behave? I'm the best behaved out of the bunch!"

They laughed together, then Laurel left Jessa to her work and wandered back to the house. Instead of going inside, she sat down on the porch swing, tucking one foot up under her. Slowly she set the swing in motion and let out a long breath.

There were only sounds of nature drifting on the warm breeze. Leaves on the nearby trees rustled as the birds chirped. She wanted the peacefulness of her surroundings to seep into her heart, but now with all the other distractions gone, the turmoil within her stirred again.

She missed Matt so much. At moments like this, if he appeared in front of her, she didn't know if she'd hug him or slap him. Not that she'd ever hit him, but she really wanted to just knock some sense into him. There was no reason to be so dead set against having children, unless there was some genetic anomaly or disease he would pass down. She was pretty sure if that had been the reason, he would have been more forthcoming with it. Instead it was just *no, I don't want children.* End of story. Unfortunately for her, it wasn't the end of the story. It was just the beginning.

By Friday, Matt knew he needed to see Laurel. It had been a week with no communication. He didn't know what he was going to say, but he needed to see her. As soon as work finished, he went home, packed a bag and set out for the three hour drive to Collingsworth.

The ride there gave him a lot of time to think about things. Not that every single day hadn't already given him that opportunity. The long hours of the evening had been solitary and lonely. Television only distracted him for so long. Thankfully, once he fell asleep, he slept soundly until his alarm went off in the morning for work. But the weekend alone held no appeal for him. So he was going to take a chance that Laurel would actually talk to him.

The longer days meant the sun was just beginning to fade as he drove through the town. The closer he got to the manor, the more nervous he became. And doubts began to creep in. Maybe it hadn't been a good idea to come. Particularly when he couldn't offer Laurel any change of heart where the baby was concerned.

He turned into the driveway, slowing to navigate the turns that led to the manor. Lights were still on downstairs, though some of the upper windows were darkened. Matt parked his truck beside the other two vehicles in front of the garage. He grabbed his bag, and before letting his nerves and second thoughts get the better of him, climbed out and headed for the front door.

He rang the doorbell and then stood waiting, wondering which of the sisters would answer. And if they would let him into the house. He hoped it would be Violet, because of all the sisters, she seemed the most likely to let him have some time with his wife.

But luck was not with him. It was Jessa who opened the door. Instead of stepping aside to let him in, she stood, one hand on her hip, the other on the door jamb blocking his way.

"What are you doing here?" she asked. Though her position seemed defensive, her tone was not.

"I'd like to see Laurel," Matt told her.

Still not moving, Jessa asked, "Have you changed your mind about the baby?"

Matt debated his answer for a split second, but knew he couldn't lie. He needed to at least show them he wasn't trying to hide things. "No."

"Then why are you here?" Jessa asked again. "You have to know she's hurting. I don't know that seeing you is what she needs right now."

"I understand that. But I...miss her so much. I just want to see her. See if we can talk."

Jessa stared at him for what felt like an eternity. Finally she moved back from the door, leaving him room to step into the foyer. "I'm not sure it's the right thing, but I'll let Laurel decide. She can kick you out if that's what she wants."

"Thank you, Jessa," Matt said, with all sincerity. "I appreciate this very much."

Jessa nodded with her head to the staircase. "She's upstairs in her room."

Matt thanked her again and headed for the stairs. Part of

him wanted to bound up the staircase two at a time, but instead he climbed step by step. There was every possibility she would kick him out like Jessa had said. He hoped that wasn't the case, but if it was, he would accept it.

Outside her room he paused for a moment before rapping lightly. After what seemed like forever, he heard her call out to come in. Matt took a deep breath and opened the door. Soft light greeted him as he stepped into the room and closed the door behind him. He saw immediately that Laurel was in bed already.

She pushed herself into a sitting position and shoved back her hair. As she spotted him, her movements froze. "Matt?"

He dropped his bag by the door, and walked toward the bed. The sight of her set his heart racing. As he got closer, he could see the redness around her eyes and the pallor of her skin. Without thinking, he reached out and cupped her cheek, rubbing his thumb across the wetness there.

Laurel didn't move at first, but then fresh tears welled up and spilled over. She jerked away from him and crawled to the other side of the bed and got out. As she stood there, hands fisted at her sides, Matt could suddenly see the changes in her body as a result of the pregnancy. The tight tank top and leggings she wore fit every curve of her body. A body he knew as well as he knew his own. Only now it was changing.

"What are you doing here?" Laurel asked, her voice soft. She swiped at the fresh tears on her cheeks.

"I needed to see you," Matt said. "I missed you."

"Have you changed..." Laurel's words faded as she swallowed hard.

Matt wished he could lie to her even more than he had wanted to lie to Jessa. But if anyone deserved the truth, it was this beautiful woman in front of him. "No."

Her face crumpled at the word, and she covered her face with her hands. Her soft weeping cut into his heart. Why couldn't he just say yes? Just say it would be okay to have the baby. Maybe he wasn't like his dad. He hadn't lost his temper in ages. And he'd never lost it with Laurel.

But the one time you really lost it, someone died, the little voice in his head reminded him. All it would take was one time. And he had heard guys at work talk about how difficult that first year was with an infant. No sleep. Crying, colicky baby. Stress levels high. And then came the terrible twos and threes. Yeah, he'd heard the horror stories. It just sounded so much like a recipe for disaster for someone like him.

Matt rounded the bed and took her into his arms. He closed his eyes as he held her for the first time in what felt like forever. If he couldn't last a week without holding her, how was he going to live the rest of his life?

He picked her up in his arms and laid her on the bed before walking to her side to snap off the lamp. He took off his socks and shoes and then crawled into the bed next to her, still wearing his jeans and t-shirt. Though he'd missed their physical intimacy, that wasn't why he'd come.

When he gathered her into his arms again, she didn't pull away, but she also didn't stop crying. He held her, stroked her back, but had no words to ease her pain. He understood it, what she was grieving for. It was a grief he felt so much himself. But there was nothing either of them could do to change it. She wouldn't give up the baby, and he just couldn't take a chance of hurting her or their child.

Eventually her weeping subsided, and he felt the tension ebb from her body. He tucked her head under his chin and closed his eyes, praying that sleep would come quickly.

Laurel woke with the urgent need to go to the bathroom. The immediate feeling of being trapped slipped away as memory returned. *Matt.* She could hear his steady even breathing as he held her. Though she hated to have to wake him, she needed to go to the bathroom. Soon.

Moving as slowly as she could, Laurel shifted out of his embrace and over to the edge of the bed.

"Where you going?" Matt's voice was low and rough in the darkness.

"Just have to go to the bathroom." She stood up and made her way to the closed door that led to the bathroom she shared with Violet. She opened it and flicked on the light before closing the door behind her.

After she finished, Laurel washed her hands and stared at herself in the mirror. She looked an absolute wreck. Her eyes were red and sore, and the dark circles under her eyes were more pronounced than ever. Shutting down all the voices in her head telling her that crawling back into that bed with Matt was a bad idea, Laurel went back into her room.

Matt had turned on the lamp on his side of the bed and was standing with his back to her going through a bag. He turned around and held up a pair of shorts. "Jeans aren't exactly the most comfortable thing to sleep in."

Laurel nodded and sat down on her side of the bed, facing away from him. They had never been shy about changing in front of each other before, but right then, given the future that seemed to lie ahead, it felt wrong for her to watch him. And yet she knew that when he laid back down in her bed, she would be right there with him.

The bed moved as he joined her again. He snapped off the light, plunging them into darkness. Laurel lay back down, still facing away from Matt. For a moment they lay in silence, not moving then slowly she shifted toward the middle of the bed. Matt met her there and pulled her into him, his front warm against her back. It was one of her favorite ways to sleep with him. She always felt so safe and secure in his arms.

His hand skimmed her hip and settled on her stomach. It was how they normally slept in this position, but this time, as his hand touched her, she tensed. Though it wasn't noticeable to anyone when she wore normal clothes, Laurel was aware of the growing bump in her abdomen. And she knew that Matt felt it too. His hand lifted, and then settled back down again, cupping the small bump. Laurel felt hot tears slip from her eyes as she slid her hand over the back of his and intertwined their fingers.

And she allowed herself to slip from the ugly reality into the place where Matt was happy about this baby, and they were eagerly awaiting his or her arrival in their lives. It was the one place from which she could slip into sleep without crying. It was a dangerous place to go to though, because it kept a fruitless hope alive. But she just wanted it so bad, and to have Matt there now, feeling the baby as only he could, and not reject it or her, fanned that flame of hope like nothing else could.

❧ Chapter Ten ❧

*F*OR the second time that night, Matt felt Laurel fall asleep in his arms. As he laid there, his hand pressing against one of the physical changes he had noticed about her earlier, Matt wondered what this child would be like. Would it inherit his anger problem? Even if it did, he knew Laurel would raise it in such a way that the anger wouldn't tear at this child's life the way his father's anger had or the way his had and well might again.

Every single time he thought of maybe, just maybe, telling Laurel he'd stay with her and this baby, fear literally squeezed the breath from his body. He would never abandon his financial responsibility for the child, but as long as this fear held him in its grip, there was no chance he could be there in any other way.

He slept fitfully the rest of the night. Finally around seven he moved away from Laurel. She shifted in her sleep but didn't waken. He wondered if she was still suffering from morning sickness. It amazed him how well she'd managed to hide it from him during the last few weeks they'd been together.

He moved across the room without turning any lights on and made his way downstairs. The light was already on in the kitchen, and he spotted Violet sitting at the breakfast nook, a Bible open in front of her and a mug cupped in her hands.

Knowing his bare feet wouldn't make any noise, Matt cleared his throat as he walked into the room.

Violet glanced around, her eyes widening in surprise. "Matt?"

"Morning," he said. "Coffee smells good."

"Help yourself," Violet told him with a wave of her hand in the direction of the coffee maker. "What are you doing here?" She pushed back from the table and came to sit on one of the high stools at the counter. "Is everything okay with you and Laurel?"

For the third time in less than twelve hours, Matt had to once again say no. "I just needed to see her."

"And she didn't ask you to leave?" Violet asked.

Matt shook his head. "I'm sure she thought about it though."

Violet didn't say anything as she took a sip of coffee, but her concern was clearly written across her face.

"Does she usually have something she eats or drinks in the morning to help with the morning sickness?" he asked.

"You're going to make this harder for her, you know," Violet said. "Being nice to her."

"I can't be anything *but* nice to her. I love her."

"But you can't be with her," Violet stated.

"No, I can't. For her sake and the baby's. I just can't."

"Why?" Violet set her cup down on the counter. "Laurel hasn't really said anything about why, just that it has something to do with a deal you guys made before you got married."

"Yes, we agreed on no children."

"But why? Most people don't decide so young to not have children without a valid reason."

Matt stared at his sister-in-law. He set his cup of coffee down on the counter. "I'll be right back."

He walked out into the brisk morning air, without shoes, to his truck. Thankfully he hadn't locked it the night before, so he could grab the file he'd placed in the front seat a couple of nights ago. He stood there for a moment with it in his hand wondering if this was the best decision. But maybe, if he could get Violet to understand, she could help Laurel.

Back in the kitchen, he laid the file on the counter in front of Violet. "Before you read that, tell me what I need to make for Laurel."

Violet got up and went to a cupboard and handed him a package of tea. "I know she's been drinking that to help with it. And usually she eats a piece of toast."

"Just plain?"

"With a little butter, I think."

Matt nodded and took the bread from Violet and put a couple of slices into the toaster. While he waited for it, he heated up some water in the microwave and put a tea bag in it. Violet had returned to her seat but hadn't touched the file.

"There's a tray in the pantry," she told him when he looked around for something to put the plate and cups on.

"Thank you." Matt topped up his coffee and then added it to the tray where Laurel's tea and toast waited. "When you're done with that, please don't leave it lying around. I wouldn't want Lily or Rose to get their hands on it."

Violet's brow furrowed as her gaze dropped to the file. Matt turned and headed out of the kitchen. He'd left the door open a crack when he'd gone down earlier, so he used his elbow to push it open further. Light spilled from the bathroom, and he could hear the sounds of Laurel being sick. Moving as quickly as he could with the tray, he set it down on the bed and went to the bathroom.

He knelt down beside her, gathering her hair back from her face with one hand and rubbing her back with the other. Last time she'd pulled away, this time she let him minister to her and be there to support her. When it finally eased, she leaned sideways against him. He felt her take a deep breath and let it out. He would have liked to stay there and hold her forever, but he struggled to breathe without wanting to throw up himself.

Laurel allowed him to help her to her feet. "Just give me a minute."

Matt was more than willing to vacate the bathroom. He turned on the light on her side of the bed and had just picked up his coffee when she reappeared. "I got you some tea and toast. Violet said it's what you like in the morning."

Laurel walked slowly to the bed and sank down on it. She looked up at him and gave him a weak smile. "Thanks."

He handed her the mug first, figuring she might like something to replace the liquids she'd just had drained from her body. She took it with both hands and lifted it to take a small sip.

"Is it still really bad?" Matt asked as he sat down beside her on the bed.

"When I get it, yes. But it's been changing a bit since I've been here. I don't have it every morning anymore. But now it seems to strike whenever. Usually still in the morning, but it can come anywhere from five o'clock to ten o'clock."

"Even though it's been just a week, there are other changes I see," Matt told her.

Laurel tugged her tank top from her chest and glanced sideways at him. Matt gave her a lopsided grin and a wink. "Yes, those and your stomach."

Laurel blushed, but as her hand slid down to rest on her abdomen, her expression sobered. When she looked back up at him, her eyes were bright with unshed tears. "Please? Is there no way you can make this work? I need you. *We* need you." Her voice was soft, but every word struck him like an arrow.

He shouldn't have come. Matt stood and moved away from the bed. He really shouldn't have come. It had been a selfish move on his part. He set his mug down on the night stand and left the room. Downstairs he found Violet sitting once again at the breakfast nook. Her head was bent, but her hand rested on his closed file.

As before, he cleared his throat to alert her to his presence. She moved more slowly this time. Lifting her head, she picked the file up. When she stood and turned toward him, Matt saw emotions rampant on her face. Sadness was the one that stood out most to him though. He held out his hand for the folder. She gripped it flat against her chest.

Violet shook her head. "Don't show it to her."

"I have to," Matt told her. "She needs to know. She needs to understand."

"You shouldn't have come," Violet said. "This is just going to leave her even more broken. Don't do this to her. Hope is all she has right now."

"It's hope for nothing, Violet. Do you think it's fair for me to let her keep that hope?"

"No more than it's fair for you to come to her, sleep in her bed, treat her nicely and then give her this." Anger flared in Violet's gaze. She lifted the file in one hand and shook it. "This does not have to define you, Matt. You could rise above this. In fact, I think you already have."

"All it takes is one time," Matt said. "You know the stresses that come with children. They are all things that can set off a person like me. Do you really want your sister and niece or nephew to be around when that happens?"

"*If* it happens," Violet corrected him. "There's no guarantee it ever would."

"And there's no guarantee it wouldn't. Is that a chance you're willing to take with her life? With the baby's? And Rose's? There is just too much at stake for me to take that chance." Matt held out his hand for the folder again. This time she handed it to him.

"I still think you're making a mistake. With all of this." He took one edge of the file, but she kept her grip on the other, forcing him to look at her. "Have you prayed about this? Do you feel peace about this decision? Do you not trust God to help you with the anger?"

"I don't feel peace about anything, Violet. None of the options I have give me any peace. But this is the one decision I can live with because I know Laurel and the baby will be safe."

Violet let the file slide from her grip, and Matt turned to go. His steps were heavy as he climbed the stairs to the second floor and the room where Laurel waited for him.

It appeared she hadn't moved at all since he'd left. Her head lifted as he walked into the room. There was no hope on her face, only resignation. Even the tears had dried.

"I'm going to go," he told her. "I shouldn't have come. It was very selfish of me."

Laurel nodded, as if she had known this was coming. "Though it has made things more difficult, part of me is glad you came."

He laid the folder beside his bag and shoved his jeans into it before zipping it shut. After he put on his socks and shoes, he picked up the file again. Violet's words played in his mind, but Laurel deserved to know the truth now. All of it.

When he turned around, he found her watching him, sadness etched on her face. It made him want to cry, but instead he approached her and held out the file.

She looked at it, then back up at him. "Divorce papers?"

Matt reared back. It took him off guard because even though he knew there was no future for them, he hadn't considered divorce. He quickly shook his head. "No. Not divorce papers. This will help you understand why I feel the way I do about children. I just need you to understand. I think it will make it easier for both of us."

"Nothing will ever make this easier," Laurel said. At first she didn't take the folder, but when he continued to hold it out to her, she reached out and he let it slip into her hand.

"Take care of yourself. Call me if you need anything. Anything at all."

Laurel bit her lip as she nodded. Matt wanted to hug her and kiss her, but knew that would just make this hard parting even more difficult. He turned, picked up his bag and headed for the door. As he grasped the doorknob, he glanced back over his shoulder to where Laurel sat.

She was still looking at him and when their gazes met she said, "I love you, Matt. I always will, but please don't come back."

Matt nodded but didn't say anything. Not because he didn't want to, but because his vocal cords had tightened painfully in an attempt to keep from breaking down. He passed the entrance to the kitchen without entering it this time and let himself out. He didn't allow himself to pause or stop at all, knowing that once he did, he might never go. He got into the truck, started it right up, reversed out of the spot he'd parked in and drove away from the manor.

Away from the only woman he would ever love.

ॐ

Laurel looked up as her bedroom door burst open. Violet stood there, a frown on her face.

"He left? Did I just hear him leave?" She walked over to the bed, and Laurel saw her gaze go to the folder she held in her lap. "Don't read that."

Of all the things she'd expected Violet to say, that hadn't been it. "He told me to."

"I know he wants you to, but it's…hard to read. To look at."

"I have to, Violet," Laurel told her firmly. "I owe it to Matt to at least look through it."

"You owe Matt nothing," Violet said as she slashed her hand through the air, anger tightening her features. "He's abandoned you."

Laurel shook her head. "This pregnancy wasn't something I planned, but I did know Matt never wanted children. My choice to keep the baby and not abort or give it up for adoption is my decision. He knows why I won't give up the baby. Now I need to understand why he can't accept this child of ours."

Violet's hands clenched. "Can I just tell you what's in the file?"

"You read it?"

"Matt gave it to me when he came down to get you breakfast."

"No, I need to do this. For the first time Matt is being completely open about what happened to bring him to this point. I want to know that."

Violet gave a shake of her head, resignation on her face. "Fine, but don't say I didn't warn you."

"I appreciate your concern. I do. But I need to do this."

"I'll be downstairs if you want to talk," Violet said before spinning on her heel and leaving the room.

Laurel knew her sister was angry at Matt, but right then anger wasn't something there was room for in her heart. Maybe in a few days that would come, but right then it was just sadness and grief.

File in hand she crawled to the center of the bed and sat cross-legged. She laid the file down in front of her and after blowing out a quick breath, she opened it.

The headline of the aged newspaper jumped out at her. *Ten-year-old kills father.*

೫ Chapter Eleven ೫

LAUREL picked it up and looked at the date. The paper was seventeen years old. The names in the article were not familiar to her immediately, but then she recognized Steven's last name. The article touched on possible abuse by the father. Of it being self-defense. A sinking sense of dread settled into her stomach. Slowly she set aside the article and moved on. As she read through the police reports and looked at the photos of the crime scene, photos of a scared, bruised and bloodied little boy who looked an awful lot like Matt, hopelessness joined the dread in her stomach.

Notes made by detectives in charge of the case regarding how the mother wouldn't back up her son's story. Nor would the boy's older brother. Then came the foster home reports. Note after note of fights he'd gotten into. Counsellors went on record to say he needed more help to control his anger. When Laurel got to the last page, she knew it was about Matt because that last document was the one he'd received when he'd legally changed his name to the one she shared with him.

But none of what she read seemed to jive with the man

she knew now. She hadn't seen the anger the psychologists and counsellors had made note of. Never had he raised his voice to her, let alone a hand. She just couldn't reconcile them in her mind. But if this was the ugliness in his past that had brought him to the point of not wanting children of his own, she now understood. Unfortunately, it changed nothing. She still had a child growing within her that she refused to give up, and he couldn't accept that.

Laurel put all the pictures back into the file. She got up, used the bathroom, pulled the curtains tightly closed, turned off the light and crawled back into bed. As she lay in the darkness, she prayed, talked to the baby and prayed some more.

As the day wore on, she didn't bother to get up except to get a drink or use the bathroom. Her mind was in turmoil, and she really didn't want input from Violet or Jessa right then. Their perspective of Matt and the situation was lacking one important thing that she had and they didn't. Love. They didn't know him like she did. Violet knew about the ugliness of his past, but she'd never experienced the beauty that was Matt now. Laurel had. Her heart grieved for the young boy who'd been betrayed by those who should had loved him without question. The hurt had gone far beyond the fists of a father to the heartless rejection by a mother...the mother he had no doubt been trying to protect.

She drifted off to sleep at some point and woke to find a tray with a sandwich on it. Though she was far from hungry, mindful of the baby, Laurel managed to eat half of it, then went back to sleep again. In her dreams was happiness. Love won. And they were all together. Waking to the dark reality she now faced was hard.

But when the sun rose the next morning, Laurel got out of bed. She took a shower and even put on some makeup before going downstairs to go to church with the others. It was time for her to reach deep and find the strength she needed to go forward. She had been weak for too long now and the baby and Rose both needed her to be strong. The endless crying and dwelling on her hopeless situation had to end. For the sake of her children, she would go on. And one of the steps of going forward was telling Rose who she really was. And she wanted to do that as soon as she could.

"Are you sure you're ready for whatever her response might be?" Jessa asked. "I know you're dealing with an awful lot right now. There's no guarantee she'll react positively."

"I know, but she needs to know. She needs to know I'm her mother, and that I love her."

Jessa nodded. "I've been praying about this, so if you feel it's the right time, I will support you."

"Thank you." Laurel gave her a hug. "Can I tell her by myself?"

Again Jessa nodded. "I'll give you guys some space."

"I think I'd like to walk down to the shore with her."

Jessa went to find Rose while Laurel got her shoes from her room.

"Do you want to come for a walk with me, Rosie?" Laurel asked when she found them in the kitchen.

Rose lit up. "Yes! Where are we going?"

"I thought we'd walk down by the lake."

Rose grinned. "I can show you how I skip rocks. Violet's been teaching me."

"She's always been better at that than any of the rest of us."

Once Rose had her shoes on, they went out the back door. Laurel held out her hand and felt her heart clench as Rose took it. Clasped hands swinging between them, they walked down the dirt path that led to the water's edge. Many years ago Gran had had a swing brought down and had often come down to end the day at the water's edge.

Once there, Rose showed her how well she could skip rocks. Laurel tried to follow her lead, but failed miserably.

"Violet eventually gave up trying to teach me," Laurel told her with a smile. "I'm going to sit on the swing. Want to come and swing for a bit?"

Rose followed her to the wooden swing structure. They settled side by side on the heavy wood seat. Laurel set the swing in motion with her foot, wondering how to broach the subject.

"I heard Violet talking to Jessa about you," Rose said.

Laurel glanced over at the little girl, wondering if she would have to broach the subject after all. "What about?"

"That you're having a baby. Is it true?" Rose asked, curiosity in her blue eyes.

Laurel nodded. "Yes, I'm having a baby."

Rose's gaze dropped to her stomach. "Do you know if it's a boy or a girl?"

"Not yet. I'll have to wait a little while to find that out."

"Are you happy about it?" Rose asked.

"Yes, I'm happy about it."

"But Matt isn't?"

Laurel wondered just what type of conversation Rose had heard, but decided she needed to be honest. "Matt doesn't think he'll be a good father. He never wanted a baby."

"So are you going to leave the baby here? Like our mom did?"

The question shocked Laurel. She quickly shook her head. "No, this baby will stay with me."

The corner of Rose's mouth lifted. "Then the baby will be

lucky."

Laurel wasn't sure how to proceed from that point, but decided to just push on. "Rose, do you remember how Gran was?"

"You mean how she was really strict and kinda mean sometimes?"

"Yes, she could be that way. She was also very worried about how people would see our family if we made mistakes. Like my mom. Every time she got pregnant, she brought the baby back here for Gran to raise. It was hard for Gran to deal with everyone knowing her only daughter kept making mistakes."

"Are we mistakes?"

Realizing that perhaps she'd used the wrong word, Laurel struggled with finding the right one. "In Gran's eyes, Mama getting pregnant without being married was a mistake. A big one. A mistake she kept making. But no, in God's eyes, and mine, none of us are mistakes, but the choices that Mama made that led to our births weren't good ones. Then one of us made the same choice as our mom."

"Someone got pregnant without being married?"

Laurel nodded. "And Gran was very angry. She didn't want people to think another family member was going to turn out like Mama. So when that baby was born, Gran took it away and said that Mama had had another baby."

Rose's face showed her confusion.

Laurel sent up a quick prayer, asking God to help her. "The thing is, Rose. It was me who got pregnant without being married. Gran then sent Cami and me away for a year. During that year, I had a baby girl who Gran brought back to Collingsworth, and then told everyone she was Mama's baby. By the time we came back, everyone just believed what Gran wanted them to. No one ever guessed I was the baby's mother. And though I really wanted that baby to be mine, Gran wouldn't let me have her. She said she'd be better growing up at Collingsworth than with me. So I let her have her way, but now Gran's gone, and I want my baby back."

Rose didn't say anything right away. She sat staring out at the water, and Laurel wondered if it was just too much for a ten year old to be able to grasp, even though Rose seemed more mature for her age than most ten year olds.

Finally Rose turned and looked at her. The young girl's gaze searched her face, as if looking for similarities that would support what Laurel was saying. "Am I that baby? Cause Lily is too old."

Laurel nodded. "Yes, you are my baby, Rose."

There was no immediate change of expression on her face, but then slowly a smile curled the edges of her mouth and light began to glow in her eyes. "You're my mom?"

"Yes." Laurel tried hard to keep from crying. As much as she wanted this baby growing inside her, she wanted this baby who had been taken away from her ten years earlier.

"And you want me?"

"Oh, you bet. I've wanted you from the day you were born, but Gran didn't want me to have you. And then I wasn't sure if I should tell you or not."

"Will I come live with you? Will Matt be my dad?"

It was like a knife plunged in her heart, but Laurel managed not to cry at the pain. "Yes, you will live with me. Unfortunately, Matt and I aren't together anymore."

Rose's brows drew together. "You're getting divorced?"

"Not right away. But we just can't be together right now."

"Because of the baby?" Rose gestured to her stomach. "And because of me?"

"Not because of you, sweetheart. And not because of the baby either. Matt has some things he needs to work through. And maybe he won't ever be able to work through them. But neither you nor this baby is to blame for how things have worked out between us." Laurel reached out to pull Rose close. "Don't ever think that."

Rose wrapped her arms around Laurel and hugged her tightly. They sat that way for several minutes, and Laurel couldn't keep the tears from flowing.

When Rose looked up and saw them, she reached out and brushed them from Laurel's cheeks. "Why are you crying?"

"Because I'm so happy you want me to be your mom. And because I'm so sad that I can't give you a dad too."

"It's okay. I thought I didn't have a mom or dad, but now I have a mom. I'm happy about that."

Laurel took her face in her hands and pressed a kiss to her forehead. "I'm happy about that too."

When they walked into the kitchen a little while later, Jessa was sitting at the counter, her laptop open in front of her. As soon as she spotted them, she stood and smiled.

"Everything okay?" she asked.

"Laurel's my mom!" Rose told her excitedly.

"I know, sweetheart. Are you happy about that?"

Rose nodded. "She's gonna be mom to me and the baby."

"And she's gonna be a great mom," Jessa said. Tears shimmered in her eyes as she met Laurel's gaze. As she pulled her close for a hug she softly said, "I'm so glad this went well for you."

Needing something to distract her, Laurel asked Rose if she wanted to make some cookies. The little girl happily agreed and scampered around gathering the ingredients

Laurel listed off to her.

They had just stuck the final cookie sheet in the oven when Violet walked in with Dean and Addy. They accepted the cookies Laurel and Rose offered them. Once the last batch of cookies was done, Rose asked if she could take Addy to her room to play. Given permission, the two girls ran from the room and raced up the stairs.

"Listen, Laurel, I know you probably don't want to rehash this Matt stuff, but I thought maybe you would be interested in what Dean has to say."

Laurel sat down at the table where the other three were. "I don't mind talking about it, but not if everyone is going to try to solve the problem. The only one who can change things now is Matt."

Dean cleared his throat and leaned forward. "I was part of Matt's case."

Laurel looked at him in surprise. "You were?"

"I was a rookie, and Tom, my partner, and I, were one of the first cars to arrive on the scene." Dean's gaze drifted out the window, and Laurel knew it wasn't the scenery he was seeing at that moment. "When we walked in, the first thing his mother said was 'he did it.' And he just stood there, knife still in his hand."

"Was he hurt?" Laurel asked. She'd seen the pictures so she knew what the answer was, but she still had to ask.

Dean nodded, and his gaze came back into focus on her. "Yes, his body was covered in bruises and x-rays later showed old fractures to his arms. Even his mother was bleeding and had broken fingers on her one hand. There was no doubt the father had been beating them all, and it had not just happened for the first time that night."

"He never told me anything about what happened back then," Laurel said, her fingers shredding a napkin on the table. "I guess he was trying to protect me."

"Honestly, I was surprised when Violet told me who Matt was. I had wondered off and on through the years what had happened to him. Once he was out of the foster care system, there were no more reports on him. I suppose I could have tracked him down, but I didn't. I guess he changed his name at some point."

"Yes, the year before we met, he changed his last name," Laurel told him.

"I'm going to give you my opinion on this, for what it's worth. Keep in mind I have years of experience dealing with people who have come from backgrounds like Matt's, but I don't have a psychology degree or anything like that." Dean glanced at Violet then back to Laurel. "I'm very surprised that this is how Matt turned out. Statistics show a large percentage of people coming from an abusive background like what he had will go on to be abusers themselves."

"His brother is," Laurel said, her mind going back to that night in the hospital.

Dean's eyebrows rose. "You've met his brother?"

"Briefly. For some reason he called Matt when he took his wife to the hospital for injuries he inflicted on her. The cops got involved, and he was not very happy with Matt because he wouldn't take his side."

"That's the outcome typically expected from their sort of background. Matt was definitely on that track, as I'm sure you saw when you read his foster care reports."

Laurel nodded. There had been blacked out spots on the reports, but enough had still been showing to give a good idea of what was going on. "He got into a lot of fights and was moved around a lot."

"Something changed though because the path he was on didn't lead to where he is today."

Laurel thought back over conversations she'd had with Matt over the years. "I think it might have something to do with Devon, his best friend. I know he says it was his family who introduced him to church where he became a Christian."

Dean nodded, a thoughtful look on his face. "Well, if there is one thing that could change someone so drastically, it would be God."

"But none of this changes Matt's feelings," Laurel pointed out. "He is still dead set against having children. I wish he could see that he's come so far already. I think he could handle having a baby in the mix. Especially now that I know his past, it would help me to help him."

"Do you know if he's ever taken any anger management courses?" Violet asked.

"Not that I'm aware of, but he could have gone to some before we met." Laurel sighed. "I just wish I could get him to see this could work."

"He's going to have to come to that conclusion," Dean told her. "He needs that confidence in himself in order for it to work. You can't always be the buffer between him and the things that might upset him. Especially if it's a child. Right now he has no confidence he'll be able to control his anger around a child. I'm pretty sure he's seen the statistics. That's probably what made him press for that deal before you guys got married."

Laurel tilted her head and look at Dean. "Do you think there's any chance he'll come around? Gain that confidence you say he needs?"

"There's always a chance," Dean assured her. "And with God in the picture, well, the impossible is possible."

"I'm wondering if I should phone his friend and tell him what's happened. I'm pretty sure he hasn't shared any of this with anyone. Maybe Devon could help him out." Laurel bit her lip. "I'm worried about him. We are best friends. We do...did so much together. Now he's alone. I have all you guys and Rose, but he has no one right now. I want Devon to know so at least someone is there for him."

"I think that's probably a good idea," Violet said. "And he might be a good voice of reason."

They talked a bit longer, but then Laurel excused herself to go call Devon. Once the idea came to her, it wouldn't leave her alone.

Upstairs in her room she sat down on the bed and found Devon's name in her contact list. He answered immediately.

"Hi, Devon. It's Laurel."

"Hey, Laurel! How's it going?" Devon asked.

From Devon's tone it was fairly obvious he hadn't spoken with Matt. "Not so good, I'm afraid."

There was a pause on the other end of the line then Devon spoke in a much more serious tone. "Is something wrong with Matt?"

"He's fine. Physically. It's just that I thought you should know we separated last week."

"Separated?" Even over the phone Laurel could hear the incredulity in his voice. "This is a joke, right? I mean, I know you've been having some issues. Matt shared some of it with me at the retreat, but I didn't think it was this serious. "

Laurel sighed. "I wish it weren't. Something happened that Matt just couldn't accept."

Another pause. "You're pregnant?"

Laurel was a bit surprised that Matt had told Devon about their deal. "Yes, I found out about a month ago, but just told Matt last week. He didn't take it well."

"I can imagine. I saw him at church this morning, but he didn't say anything about this. He looked a little rough around the edges, but he said he was working hard and that you were visiting your sisters in Collingsworth."

"That's true, I am here with them. And I'm sure he's working hard, but yes, we're separated. I'm calling because I think Matt needs someone. He came here Friday night and before he left yesterday morning, he gave me a file. It was filled with everything from his past."

"You didn't know any of it?" Devon seemed surprised.

"No. He'd just told me he'd had a rough childhood and didn't like to dwell on it. He said his dad was dead, and he'd lost contact with his mom. I did meet his brother a couple of weeks ago though."

"Steven? He's bad news."

"Yeah," Laurel agreed and told him a little about the circumstances under which she'd met him. "He went ballistic on Matt when Matt wouldn't stand up for him with the cops."

"I assume you want me to try to change Matt's mind about the baby?" Devon asked.

"If I thought you could, I would ask you to, but I really don't think anyone but God can do that now. I just want someone there for him. I know he's hurting as badly as I am through this. I have my sisters, but he doesn't have anyone."

"He has me," Devon assured her. "Thank you for calling. I'll get in touch with him right away and see what I can do for him."

"Take care of him, please. I love him so much." Laurel's voice cracked as she spoke.

"I will. I'll give you a call if something comes up that I think you need to know."

"Thank you. Say hi to Amy for me."

After she hung up, Laurel lay flat back on her bed, staring

at the ceiling. She hoped she'd done the right thing. She really did want someone to be there for Matt. And, yes, there was a small part of her that hoped maybe Devon could get him to see reason. She wondered what Matt prayed when he prayed about their situation. Did he pray she'd be willing to give the baby away? Or that something would happen with the pregnancy? She couldn't imagine that, knowing him as she did, but what else could he pray for if he wanted things to change when he wasn't willing to reconsider his position?

❧ Chapter Twelve ☙

MATT emptied another garbage can into the black bag he held. The house was slowly spiraling into a pig-sty without Laurel there to keep order. He'd always helped out, but she was definitely the driving force in keeping order in their home. After dragging himself to church that morning, he'd figured he might as well fill the day with a bunch of other things he didn't want to do.

After gathering up the garbage he went through all the mail that had piled up, setting aside things that looked important. He was surprised there weren't more bills, but figured Laurel must get most of them electronically. As he sat at the table, papers in hand, Matt realized they needed to deal with the logistics of this situation. Everything was tied together. They had a joint banking account. Both their names were on the mortgage of the house. The vehicles were the only thing they each held separately. Bills still needed to be paid, and while Laurel had done all that before, it wasn't fair to expect her to continue to take care of everything now.

Matt scooped the papers back up and set them on the counter. He'd deal with them later. As he stood in front of the fridge trying to figure out what to have for supper, the doorbell rang. Frowning, Matt closed the fridge and headed for the front door.

He jerked the door open, planning to tell whoever was there he didn't want what they were peddling. Instead, he froze in surprise when he saw Devon standing on the front step.

"Hey! What are you doing here?" Matt asked.

"Laurel called me," Devon said. "Can I come in?"

Matt nodded and stepped back to let his friend into the house. "Don't mind the mess. Laurel was obviously the one who kept things afloat around here."

Matt led the way into the living room. He piled up the blankets and pillows onto the end of the couch and motioned for Devon to sit down. "I suppose she called to ask you to try to change my mind."

Devon shook his head. "Actually, she said she loved you and was worried about you being alone."

At the words, Matt swallowed hard. "I'm doing okay."

Devon glanced around the room, his gaze falling on the pile of bedding Matt had moved. "We're best friends, buddy. I am not here to lecture or judge you for what's happened. I want to support you and be a sounding board if you need to talk. Like Laurel, I love you, and I am just crushed at what has happened with you two."

"She told you she was pregnant?" Matt asked.

"Yes. Or rather, she said something had happened that you couldn't accept, and I guessed what it was."

"You know my past. You know why I feel this way. I can't change all that just because she got pregnant. Don't you think I wish I could be the father she wants for this baby?"

Devon lapsed into silence for a minute then sighed. "You know, these fears you have aren't just specific to you. I'm going through some of them myself."

"What?" Matt glanced at his friend. "Is Amy pregnant too?"

Devon nodded. "We found out this week. I think she's just about a month along. But I'm scared, man. We've wanted this. We've prayed about it, but now that it's a reality, I'm scared. It's going to mean big changes for us. Like you two, we've enjoyed being a twosome. Being able to pick up and go at the drop of a hat. Lots will change. And I hope I'm going to be able to roll with it."

"I understand that, but is one of the things you're scared about that you'll snap and beat your child?"

Devon had the grace to shake his head without hesitation. "I know that's your fear, but I honestly don't think it would happen."

"I'd love to have your confidence." Matt leaned forward, resting his elbows on his knees. "How can you be so sure?"

"Because of God. There's a verse in the Bible that talks about how if a person is in Christ, he is a new creation. The old is gone, the new has come. You changed when you became a Christian. And I believe part of the change is that God has given you freedom from the anger. Or at the very least, He has given you the ability to control it. In our weakness, He is strong. We don't have to do it all by ourselves."

Matt realized he'd never thought of God taking away his anger. In the past few years he'd had fewer outbursts, but he had attributed that to maturing and to a change in how he lived his life. No longer frequenting bars or hanging out with friends who tended to get physical after a few beers. Was it possible his anger really was gone? He just couldn't believe that was possible.

Long after Devon had left, the words still lingered in Matt's mind. *A new creation.* He wanted to believe it was true, but what if the anger was just dormant, not gone. Just lying in wait for the perfect storm of circumstances to erupt once again.

Finally, as he lay on the couch, Matt closed his eyes and pleaded for God to give him a test. To send along something that in the past would have sent him into a rage, to see what would happen. It was the only way he'd be willing to take a chance with Laurel, Rose and the baby. Now he'd just have to wait and see if God really answered prayers.

❧

"I'll try my best to be back before your bedtime, sweetie," Laurel told Rose the following Wednesday.

"Can't I come with you?" Rose asked.

"Not this time. I have a doctor's appointment and then some errands to run. I'll try to arrange a trip for us sometime this summer, okay?"

Rose wrinkled her nose, but nodded. Laurel pressed a kiss to her forehead. "Be good for Jessa."

"We'll be fine as always," Jessa said with a smile. "Drive safely."

Laurel got behind the wheel of her car, not relishing the three hour drive to the Twin Cities, but it was necessary. In addition to the doctor's appointment, she needed to stop by the house to get a few things. She hoped Matt was working because she wasn't sure she was up to seeing him. The last few days she had finally gotten to a place of reluctant acceptance that, at least for now, this was how things had to be. Now was the time to focus on Rose and the baby.

The doctor's visit went well, and tears welled up when she heard the heartbeat for the first time. How she wished Matt could have heard it too. That was their baby growing in her. A product of the fierce love they shared. She just couldn't believe a miracle of new life would be the thing to kill that love.

After leaving the doctor's office, Laurel went to the house. Since it was only around one o'clock in the afternoon, the chances of Matt being home were slim to none. Laurel let out a sigh of relief when there was no sign of his truck in the driveway. She sat for a moment staring at the outside of the home that had been filled with so much love and laughter for them.

Not wanting to dawdle, she grabbed her purse, got out of

the car and locked it before making her way to the front door. As soon as she stepped in and punched in the alarm code, she was struck by the less than fresh scent of the house. She set her purse on the table by the door and walked down the short hall. The living room on her right was a mess. Blankets were tangled on the couch and empty cans of soda lay scattered on the coffee table.

She turned toward the kitchen, dreading what she'd find there. Dirty dishes overflowed the sink, and empty Styrofoam takeout containers sat on the counters. It hurt her heart to see him living like this. And it hurt to see their home in such condition. She loved this house and had enjoyed taking care of it. Matt had always pitched in when she'd ask him to do things, but he'd never been one to do too much without guidance, at least on the inside of it. The yard and the outside of the house had been his domain, and he had always kept that up well.

Laurel knew she couldn't leave it this way. A glance at the clock told her she had time to make things right before he got home. Going to the fridge, she opened the freezer and pulled out a few packages of meat. After putting them in the microwave to defrost, she went to the living room and gathered up the bedding. The scent of the bath soap and cologne he wore clung to the sheets. She tried to ignore it as she carried them to the basement. Once the washer was going, Laurel returned to tackle the kitchen.

Thankfully, she loved to clean. It didn't take her long to get the dishes into the dishwasher. She set the meat packages she'd taken out on the counter and stood there for a minute to figure out what would be best to make for him. She dumped the hamburger into a pot, planning to make spaghetti sauce out of that, and then the chicken she'd bake with some herbs so he could just defrost and heat it up. The pork chops she decided to bake in a pan with a simple mushroom gravy. These were all dishes he loved, and hopefully he'd be able to make the sides to go with them without too much trouble.

And then after a brief hesitation, she pulled some butter

from the fridge. The last thing she'd make for him would be oatmeal chocolate chip cookies for the cookie jar.

Knowing she had to let the food cool before she could freeze it, she focused on getting the meat dishes cooked. Once they were all on the go, she turned her attention to the living room. She picked up all the trash and stuffed it into a large black garbage bag. Then she sprinkled some powdered freshener on the carpet before vacuuming since it looked—and smelled—like it hadn't been done at all since she'd left.

Once done there, she returned to the kitchen to check on the food and start the dough for the cookies. She figured she had until at least six before Matt got home, but her plan was to be gone by five. Not wanting to forget what she'd really come for, Laurel made her way to the bedroom. The door was closed and when she opened it, the stale air told her he hadn't been in the room much, if at all, since she'd left. Resolutely pushing aside tears, she made her way to the dresser and then to the bathroom to pick up the things she needed. She wasn't going to bother to clean in there.

Another trip downstairs to put the load into the dryer and then she gave the bathroom Matt was obviously using a good cleaning and took the dirty towels down to the washing machine. Feeling a little winded, Laurel sat down at the table and began to look through the bills that had piled up on the counter. She sorted them and made a pile to take with her. They were going to have to sort this out soon, but for now, she'd continue to do what she'd always done. It wasn't like she didn't have the time to take care of it.

As the meat dishes finished cooking, she set them on racks to cool and began baking the cookies. She heard the faint buzz of the dryer, so took the pile of bills that needed to be filed downstairs to their office and switched over the towels to dry. Upstairs she folded the bedding and put the cases back on his pillows before stacking them on the end of the couch.

As she ladled spaghetti sauce into containers on the counter, Laurel realized she felt more productive in the past few hours than she had in all the time since school let out.

She missed her home. The manor was nice, but it wasn't really home any more. Soon she needed to make some decisions about what to do. She knew she had a job in the fall, but was Minneapolis really the place she wanted to raise Rose and the baby? With the inheritance she didn't even need to work. Maybe it would be better to be close to family, especially for that first year after the baby was born. She had friends from church in the Twin Cities who would help her out, but they weren't family. If things continued as they had so far with Matt, it seemed most reasonable to move back to Collingsworth.

Staying would mean finding a new church and even some new friends. The thought of being with family was infinitely more appealing than trying to make her way on her own in Minneapolis. She'd done it once, but doing it with two children would be more difficult. Plus, she wasn't sure about uprooting Rose.

With the last of the meat dishes divided out and cooling in the storage containers, Laurel washed up the pots she'd used and did a quick mop of the floor. Once everything was done, she looked at the clock and saw it was almost five. Almost time to leave. She glanced around to make sure she hadn't missed anything. All that was left was to cover up the storage containers and put the last of the cookies into the cookie jar.

"What are you doing here?"

Laurel whipped around. Matt, looking exhausted and dirty from the day's work, stood in the doorway. His expression was guarded as he watched her. She glanced at the window, kicking herself for not noticing that it had started to rain. Obviously they'd let them go early.

"I came in for a doctor's appointment and had to pick up a few things."

"You didn't have to do all the cleaning."

Laurel turned to give the counter by the sink a wipe with the cloth she held. "You know I like to clean."

"Yes, I know, and I always appreciated that. Never really

realized how much you did until..."

She swallowed hard before turning back around. "I've put some meals for you in the freezer. They're labelled and all you have to do is make up some spaghetti noodles or a package of potatoes or rice."

"Thank you."

Laurel could see the exhaustion on Matt's drawn face. He looked like he had lost weight even in the few days since she'd last seen him. "I need to go. I promised Rose I'd be home before her bedtime."

"So you told her?" Matt asked.

"Yes. I told her Sunday afternoon."

"And she took it well?"

Laurel nodded. "Better than I expected actually."

"I'm glad."

Laurel looked up at him. "She asked if you were going to be her daddy."

Matt winced at her words. "I'm sorry."

"I explained as best I could."

Matt rubbed a hand across his face, smearing dirt on his cheek. Laurel longed to wipe it away. To send him off to the shower and then give him a back rub afterwards. She had loved taking care of him even more than she had loved him taking care of her.

"How was the doctor's appointment? Was it just routine or was something wrong?"

"Just routine." Laurel wondered if he'd wanted to hear that something was wrong. "I did get to hear the baby's heartbeat though."

Matt seemed at a loss as to how to react to that. Finally he just nodded.

Laurel swallowed the lump in her throat. "I'd better go."

She picked up the small bag she'd set on the kitchen table earlier. She slipped the bills into it. "I'll take care of these things when I get back to Collingsworth."

"Thank you. Again," Matt said. He stepped aside as she walked toward the entrance of the kitchen. "Drive safe."

Anxious to escape the house, Laurel nodded and grabbed her purse from the table. "Goodbye."

~ *Chapter Thirteen* ~

As soon as the door closed behind her, Matt walked into the living room to watch from the window as she pulled away from the house. He had been shocked to see her car in the driveway when he'd pulled in earlier. And then to come inside and have it smell so much like times in the past had been like a welcoming hug. Only it was clear she'd planned to be gone before he got home. It was only because of the rain that he'd arrived before she'd left.

Watching her pull away from him, Matt prayed again that God would send a test to him so he could know for sure. One way or another, he needed to know if the anger that had burned for so long within him could still overpower and strip him of all rational thought.

Looking around he noticed Laurel hadn't just cleaned up the kitchen. She must have ripped through the house like a hurricane only, instead of leaving chaos in her wake, she'd left order. His bedding sat all neatly folded and all the garbage was gone. He would have to do better with taking care of the house. He doubted she'd be back to clean up again. Although it hadn't appeared she'd taken everything she'd left behind. He was pretty sure the dresser and closet had still held more than what could fit in that small bag she'd carried.

He made his way down the hallway to the bathroom, noticing as he went that the door to their bedroom was closed. Wondering if she'd cleaned in there, he gripped the doorknob and turned it. When musty air greeted him, he realized she'd avoided the room much like he had. He closed the door and continued on to take a shower and wash the filth of the day away.

The following evening, Matt was on his way home from work when his phone rang. He pressed the Bluetooth to answer it.

"Matt, it's Melly." The woman's voice sounded strained. "Can you come help me?"

"What's wrong?" Matt asked. He was already headed in the general direction of her house, so he just continued to drive.

"I was talking to Steven...yes, I know I'm not supposed to...but he got mad and said he's on his way over here."

"Call 911, Melly. I'll get there as soon as I can, but you need to call the cops." Matt glanced over his shoulder before quickly changing lanes to get off the highway.

"I can't! He said he'd hurt me bad if I called them again. After you were here last time they showed up, but he'd already left so they didn't do anything."

"Okay, keep the doors locked and don't answer when he comes. Are the kids with you?"

"No, they're still at my mom's."

"Good. So just lock all the doors and hide. Take the phone with you."

Agreeing to do as he asked, Melly hung up the phone. Matt found a place to pull over and make a call to 911. The operator said she'd try to get a squad car sent over, but it wouldn't be high priority unless he actually showed up.

Matt hung up in disgust, hardly believing that was really

the policy the police department had regarding domestic violence. He jammed the gear shift into drive, and his tires squealed as he pulled away from the curb.

Every delay in the traffic added to his frustration. He tried calling Melly back, but there was no answer. When he finally got to the house, he threw the truck into park and turned off the ignition even as he opened the door to get out. He'd barely cleared the door when he was tackled.

"You piece of sh—" Steven's angry words hit him at the same time as his fists.

Matt raised his hands to protect his head. His brother continued to throw punches as he swore a blue streak. He shoved Matt and when he fell to the ground, Steven dropped on top of him. Matt pushed at him, trying to get free of the unrelenting blows being delivered by Steven. Finally able to scramble to his feet, Matt raised his fists, prepared to give as good as he got if his brother insisted on carrying this on.

He saw Steven rush at him but then instead of landing a punch in the man's gut, Matt stepped to the side. Steven stumbled and fell to the grass. Anger burned through Matt, but he could still think clearly and knew that fighting with Steven would only land him in trouble. He just hoped the cops showed up soon. He could see now that this had been a trap. Melly had called him, and Steven had been waiting.

"Not gonna fight, coward?" Steven taunted him. "You're not much of a man, are you?"

"The strength it's taking me not to punch your lights out right now is more than you'll ever know," Matt informed him.

Steven darted toward him. Matt stepped aside again causing his brother to lose his balance. Steven fell, and Matt could see the anger clouding everything in his brother. He saw it. He understood it. And realized he wasn't experiencing it. He was angry, yes. But it hadn't completely taken over his senses until he could no longer think rationally.

Was this the test? Even as he stood there with blood dripping from a cut from the first blows Steven had landed, hope bloomed inside him. Maybe Devon was right. Maybe he really was a changed man.

The whoop of sirens managed to pierce Steven's anger. He spun around and headed for the opening between his house and the next one. Not about to let him go, Matt lunged and tackled him like a football player. He sat on his back, keeping him trapped to the ground. The police approached with guns drawn. He lifted his hands into the air and allowed them to do what they needed to with him and Steven. The handcuffs were uncomfortable, but he knew the fastest way to get them back off was to cooperate with the police.

Steven, on the other hand, was fighting viciously with the cops. Swearing while he twisted his body in every direction, the cops had to focus their energies on trying to subdue him. Melly had come outside then, and Matt could see, even from this distance that her face was freshly bruised. He shook his head and stared down at the ground. How could you help someone who didn't want help?

Standing still, Matt looked up and saw that some of the neighbors had come out of their houses. A few approached the officers who were now free since they'd managed to wrestle Steven into the back of one of the squad cars. One woman in particular pointed at him and then at Steven. The cop seemed to be asking questions of her.

An officer approached him. "What happened here, sir?"

"I got a call from my sister-in-law," Matt said as he nodded his head in Melly's direction. "She said my brother was on his way over, and she was scared. She has a restraining order against him. I told her to call the cops and that I'd come right over. When I got here, I had barely gotten out of my vehicle when he tackled me."

"You think she set you up?"

Matt shrugged. "She can't seem to stay away from him. I was over here the other night to check on her, and he was here. After I left, I called the cops on him. I guess he wasn't too happy about that and decided to exact some revenge."

"Just wait here." The officer went to confer with a couple

of the other cops, including the one who had been talking to the neighbor.

He came back a few minutes later. Reaching around, he used a key to remove Matt's handcuffs. "The neighbor corroborated your account of what happened. We're going to run him in for violating the restraining order. If I can just get some information from you, you'll be free to go."

"How did you guys get here so fast? When I called 911 they said to call back if he showed up."

The officer jerked his head in the direction of the neighbor. "I guess the wife had told her about the restraining order, so when she saw him show up, she called 911. She was still on the phone with them when she saw you arrive and get attacked."

"Pays to have a busybody neighbor every once and a while," Matt remarked.

He glanced over to where Melly stood, her arms wrapped across her thin body, talking to another officer. He wanted to go and once again tell her to call him if she needed help, but he knew it wouldn't make any difference. Once the officer was done with him, and the squad cars began to leave, he got in his own truck and headed for home. His head hurt, and he knew he was going to have some bruises from the attack, but at least nothing was broken. And more than that, he was filled with hope. For the first time in a long time, he had hope that maybe he could be a father. A good father. Not the kind his had been.

Laurel panted as yet another wave of nausea overwhelmed her. She thought the "morning" sickness was supposed to get better as the first trimester ended. Instead, it was worse than ever. She'd been trapped in the bathroom with on and off vomiting since just after nine when she'd come upstairs to put Rose to bed. And now, almost an hour later, her abdomen was starting to hurt. No doubt she'd pulled some muscles with the horrible retching.

Eventually it eased, and she was able to drink some water and make her way back to the bed. Even though her abdomen still ached, she drifted off to sleep. A few hours later she came to full wakefulness with the urge to use the bathroom. Moving as fast as her sore body would let her, she made it to the bathroom just in time. And then she vomited again, leaving her weak and shaky.

As she crawled back into bed a little while later, she wondered if she'd picked up the flu again. This was different than her morning sickness. Even though it was difficult, she tried to sip water every few minutes until she fell asleep.

Pain shooting through her abdomen woke her again, and she immediately feared she was losing the baby.

"Oh, God, please don't take this baby," she whimpered as she curled up in pain on her bed. When the pain didn't subside, she reached for her cell phone and managed to dial Violet's number.

"Laurel?" Violet's voice sounded drowsy.

"Help me," was all Laurel was able to get out as the pain momentarily intensified.

It was barely seconds later when her door burst open, and Violet came flying in. Because she'd left her lamp on, Violet saw her immediately.

"What's wrong?" Violet asked as she knelt on the floor beside the bed. She brushed back the hair from Laurel's face.

"I don't know. I've been throwing up and now the pain is so bad."

"I think we'd better take you to the hospital," Violet said. "Let me go get Jessa. I'll be right back."

Once Violet had left, Laurel struggled to get into a sitting position. Fear for her baby was closing in around her like a dark cloud. She tried to stand, but pain prevented her from straightening.

Violet reappeared and rushed to her side. "What are you doing?"

"I need to go to the bathroom."

With Violet's help she was able to make it, and although the pain was intense, she managed to take care of herself. But her heart nearly stopped when she saw the light smear of blood on the toilet paper.

"No. No." Not wanting to believe it, Laurel flushed the toilet and called for Violet to come help her.

Violet appeared in the doorway and helped her get to the sink to wash her hands and get a drink.

"I'm spotting," Laurel told her. "I think I'm losing the baby."

"We're going to get you to the hospital before that happens," Violet told her. "Sit there while I get my stuff."

Jessa was there as well, packing a few things into a bag for her. "I'll stay here with Rose. Don't worry about anything but you and the baby."

Laurel nodded. It took both sisters to help her down the stairs and out to the car Violet had pulled up to the front of the manor.

"Phone me with any updates," Jessa said as she helped Laurel into the car. "Let me know what's going on."

"I will," Violet promised.

All the way to the hospital, Laurel kept her eyes closed trying to breathe through the pain. She couldn't believe after everything she'd gone through that God would take her baby. She'd prayed so hard for a resolution to her situation with Matt, but this wasn't the one she wanted. It was the one he had wanted, but not her.

Guess God had paid more attention to Matt's prayers than hers. Tears slid down her cheeks. Could her heart handle so much heartbreak? Right then it felt like the pain in her heart would eclipse the pain in her body.

"Hang on, sweetie," Violet said to her. "We're almost there."

✧

The ringing of his phone woke Matt. He rolled over and groaned as every place on his body where his brother had landed a punch protested the movements. He looked at the time on his phone before he answered it. *4:35*. He didn't recognize the number but answered it anyway.

"Matt?" A female voice said his name.

"Yes. Who is this?"

"It's Jessa. I thought you'd want to know that Violet has just taken Laurel to the hospital."

"What?" Matt sat straight up, the pain in his body suddenly of no significance. "What's wrong?"

"She has been vomiting off and on through the night and is in a lot of pain. Right before they left she told Violet she was spotting. She thinks she's losing the baby."

"Oh no!" Matt stood up, panic filling him. He'd just come to the place of accepting this child. Surely God wouldn't take it from them now. "I'm on my way."

"Okay. They're at the hospital in Collingsworth. I'll call you if anything else comes up."

"Thank you." Matt hung up and began to shove things into his duffle bag. He didn't know how long he'd be gone, but if he had to hang around more than a day, he didn't want to be without the things he needed.

Once on the road, he placed a call to his supervisor to let him know he wasn't going to be able to make it in. The man didn't give him any hassles since Matt had been working hard the past few weeks. He'd taken any overtime that had been offered and hadn't said no to any work he'd been asked to do. But it wouldn't have mattered if it had cost him his job; he was going to be with Laurel.

The drive to Collingsworth seemed to take twice as long as usual, but finally, just after 7:30, he was pulling into the parking lot of the hospital. Jessa had called to tell him the doctors were examining her but had no diagnosis yet.

The hospital wasn't very busy, and everyone was helpful in directing him to where Laurel was. When he got to the room, Violet spotted him and motioned for him to stay outside. He stepped back and waited. She appeared a minute later.

"Sorry. She doesn't know you're coming."

"I thought it was important I be here," Matt told her.

Violet nodded. "I agree, but I don't know how she'll react. They've finally gotten her pain under control."

"So they don't know what's wrong?" Matt asked.

"There's been mention of an ectopic pregnancy. They've tried to find the heartbeat with a Doppler but haven't been able to yet. Now we're waiting for the ultrasound to see if they can see what's wrong that way."

Matt rubbed a hand over his face. "Can I see her?"

"Yes. I'll go to the waiting room. Come get me if you need anything."

Taking a deep breath, Matt walked into the dimly lit room. As he approached the bed, he could see Laurel curled on her side, her eyes closed. Her hands were tucked up under her chin, a familiar pose. He sat down on the chair next to her bed and reached out to touch her cheek.

"Hey, babe," he spoke softly in case she was asleep.

Her eyes opened, and for a long moment she just stared at him.

"What are you doing here?" she asked.

"Jessa called me."

"She shouldn't have done that," Laurel said, closing her eyes again.

"Why? I'm your husband; this is where I should be." Matt hadn't expected this sort of reaction from her.

Her eyes flickered open. "Do you think I want you here while I struggle to hold onto something that is so important to me, but means nothing to you?"

Each word struck at Matt like a knife. "Laurel, please—"

"I guess God heard your prayers. You didn't want

children and now you won't have any." She closed her eyes again, and he saw a tear slip down her cheek. "Please leave me alone."

❧ *Chapter Fourteen* ❧

I do want the baby, Laurel. Last night I finally realized that God could help me do this."

"Easy to say now that it's not going to be an issue any more," she replied without looking at him. "Just go. If I'm going to have to grieve the loss of this child, I don't want you around while I do it."

Matt was about to protest more when a doctor walked into the room. He stopped at the end of the bed, clipboard in hand. "Are you Mr. Davis?"

"Yes." Matt stood. "Do you have any news?"

"They will be down shortly with the ultrasound to check on the baby. We're waiting for the blood results to come back from the samples drawn earlier. We still have no definitive diagnosis."

"How long will this take?" Matt felt anger rising in him. How could it take so long to figure out if she was miscarrying or not? He had thought for sure they'd know something by the time he arrived. But three hours in, and they were just finally getting around to an ultrasound?

"We are trying to rule things out and that's what the

ultrasound and blood tests will help us do. But none of these things are instant. We have been working to get her pain under control and to monitor her other vital signs. Our ultrasound technician had to finish up another scan before they could do her. We're moving as fast as we can without missing things."

Matt glanced down at Laurel. She had opened her eyes and was regarding the doctor but not saying anything. Emotions swamped him from every direction. Fear that he would lose this baby just when he'd accepted its presence in his life. Anger that things were not moving more quickly. And frustration that there was nothing he could do to help Laurel or make things move faster. He just wanted to shake the doctor to impress upon him the importance of making sure this baby and Laurel were alright.

"They should be here to do the ultrasound in about ten minutes." The doctor then asked Laurel how her pain was and checked a couple of the readings on the monitors she was hooked up to.

Once he left, Matt turned back to his wife. She looked at him with sad, but serious eyes. "Please go. Send Violet back to me."

He wanted to argue that it was his place to be there. That he *wanted* to be there for her *and* the baby. But he could see she wouldn't believe anything he said at that point. He gave a nod, turned away from the bed and headed for the door.

It didn't take long to find the waiting room. Violet was on her phone when he got there, but she quickly hung up. "Is she okay? I saw the doctor go into her room."

"They're going to do the ultrasound in about ten minutes." Matt sat down on a seat a couple of chairs down from Violet. "She told me to leave."

"What?"

"She doesn't want me there."

Violet didn't say anything, and when he looked over at her, he found her watching him, her brow furrowed. "I guess I can sort of understand that. She thinks she's losing the baby. Something that would make you happy, but is going to devastate her."

"But it won't make me happy," Matt stressed. "It's a long story, but last night I came to realize that maybe I was wrong."

"Does your revelation have something to do with the condition of your face?" Violet asked.

Matt reached a hand up to touch the cut on his forehead. "Yeah. My brother attacked me last night. It was an eye-opening encounter." He took a deep breath and blew it out. "But this is not about me now. You need to go to her. She wants you. I want to be there for her, but this is about what she wants...needs right now. But I'll be right here if anything happens."

Violet stood and placed a hand on his shoulder. "Just pray. Dean said he'd be by in a little bit, so he'll keep you company."

Matt wasn't sure he was in the mood for company right then. He was still trying to keep his anger and frustration from bubbling over. He leaned forward in the chair, elbows on his thighs, hands linked between his knees. He bent his head, trying to tune out the surrounding noise, and prayed.

Surely God wouldn't take away this baby just when he'd realized that having a child in his life wouldn't be the disaster he'd thought it would be. And if she did lose the baby, would Laurel ever believe he'd truly changed his mind about being a father? And that he had not ever prayed this baby would go away?

Time dragged. Every once in a while, he'd glance down the hallway to see if there was any movement in or out of Laurel's room. Otherwise he kept his head bent, praying harder than he'd ever prayed before.

"Matt?"

He glanced up to see Dean, wearing his sheriff's uniform, standing in front of him. Wearily Matt stood and shook the man's hand.

"Any word on how she's doing?" Dean asked.

He shook his head as he sank back down onto the chair. "Nothing."

"Is Violet with her?" Dean settled down next to him.

"Yes. Laurel didn't want me in the room," Matt told him. "They were supposed to be doing an ultrasound on her."

"Absolutely not!" The words were said by someone down the hall, but were loud enough that both men looked in that direction.

They surged to their feet when they saw Violet talking to a doctor. She was shaking her head emphatically.

Without communicating, Matt and Dean hurried to where she stood facing the doctor, her hands fisted at her sides.

"You are not sending her home," Violet informed him.

The doctor stood with his back to them. "The pain is now managed. The ultrasound showed that the baby is fine, and there has been no further spotting. There is no danger of an ectopic pregnancy."

"I understand all of that. What you don't understand is that I am not taking her out of this hospital until you can give me a definitive reason for what caused all the pain and vomiting to begin with."

The doctor shrugged. "The pain could have been caused by the excessive vomiting. And since she's already had trouble with morning sickness, it could just be a bad bout of it at a different time. As far as we can tell, there is no danger to her or the baby."

Anger swelled within Matt. How could they want to send her home with no answers? He was about to say something when Violet spoke again.

She lifted her chin and looked squarely at the doctor. "Do you know whose name is on this hospital? *Ours.* Violet Collingsworth." She poked herself with a finger and then gestured to the room where Laurel lay. "And Laurel Collingsworth-Davis. My grandmother has given generously to this hospital. If you don't want to care for my sister any more, that's fine. But she is *not* leaving this hospital without a better answer. In fact, I want to speak to another doctor. I want a second opinion."

The doctor took a step toward Violet.

"I wouldn't do that if I were you," Dean said calmly. The doctor spun around, his eyes widening as he saw Dean's uniform. "Yes, that's right. I'm the sheriff, and that's my girlfriend you're dealing with. I suggest you do as she has requested and get her that second opinion."

Matt recognized the anger flooding the man's face and understood all too well the battle he was facing at that moment. The doctor turned on his heel and set off down the hall, his white coat flapping behind him.

Violet came to Dean and leaned her head against his chest. The sheriff wrapped his arms around her. He looked down at her with a smile. "Guess the last name came in handy again, eh?"

"I hated to have to play that card, but we need some answers. And that man has been condescending and arrogant the whole time we've been here."

"Do you need to go talk to someone about another doctor?" Matt asked. "Or do you think he'll send someone?"

"I'm going to speak to someone at the nurse's station," Violet said. "I don't trust him to follow up."

They followed her to the counter behind which several nurses were talking. They looked up as the trio approached.

"I'm Violet Collingsworth, here on Laurel Collingsworth-Davis's behalf. I have just dismissed the doctor that was caring for her because he wanted to send her home without a diagnosis of what caused the pain and vomiting. I told him I wanted a second opinion, but I'm not sure if he was the correct person to make that request of."

The nurse looked at the computer screen and punched a few keys. "Ah. Dr. Albright. Let me get the supervisor for you."

It didn't take long for Violet to repeat her concerns to the nursing supervisor, and the woman assured them she would make sure a new doctor was brought in on Laurel's case. As Matt watched his sister-in-law at work, he was very grateful for her. He wasn't sure he would have been able to keep his calm and state their case as clearly as she had. Violet had always struck him as fairly easy going and laid back. To see her in this more aggressive role was eye-opening.

He looked over at Dean and saw him watching Violet with a small smile. Something told Matt this wasn't a side of his girlfriend Dean had seen much, if at all. Once the wheels were in motion for a new doctor, Violet went back to Laurel, and Dean and Matt returned to the waiting room. As he sat there, Matt realized that what he'd thought was a test last night, didn't compare to what he was struggling with today. Last night it had just been anger that had tested him. Today it was fear, helplessness and frustration that added fuel to the anger. It was taking everything within him not to lash out at someone, especially with this latest turn of events.

"I was there, you know. Did the girls tell you?" Dean said, breaking into his thoughts.

Matt sat for a moment, trying to clear his thoughts and focus on Dean. "You were where?"

"The night you killed your father. I was one of the first cops on the scene."

That grabbed Matt's attention. He turned so he could look at the man directly. "You were?"

Dean nodded. "In fact, I spoke to you, asked you if you were hurt and took the knife from you."

Matt rarely let his thoughts go back to that horrible night, but now he opened the doors to allow memories to seep in. As he did, his senses were assaulted with the memory of the sights, sounds and smells of that night. The smell of blood. And of urine. He'd wet himself at some point out of fear. He remembered his anger when he heard his mom's keening cry as his father had beat her. The pain he'd felt as his father had flung him across the room for daring to try to protect his mother. And the fear that had him scrambling to his feet as the man had stalked in his direction. Once on his feet he'd run for the kitchen and anything that would protect him. He knew if his father landed one more blow on him, it would be the last thing he ever felt.

The knife had been on the counter from where his mom had been chopping vegetables earlier. He'd picked it up in his right hand just as his dad had grabbed his left arm. With anger, fear and pain driving him, Matt had swung around, knife in hand, and plunged it into his father's chest. The man had staggered backward, the momentum pulling the knife out of his chest because of Matt's tight grip on it. But while Matt had not aimed for anything in particular, the knife had hit home, plunging deep into the man's heart. He had bled out in the time it had taken for the police and ambulance to arrive.

And Matt remembered the cop with kind blue eyes approaching him cautiously. *Dean.*

"You've come a long ways," Dean commented. "I was surprised when Violet told me who you were, and I made the connection."

"I do remember you now. That was a very...bad night." Matt stared at the floor. It felt a bit awkward to be with someone who had witnessed the worst night of his life. And here Dean was again at what was yet another very bad day for him.

"I admire you for what you've done with your life. I think you know the odds were more in favor of you turning out like your dad."

Matt nodded. "My brother did." He motioned to his face. "This is his handiwork from last night."

Dean rested a hand on his shoulder. "Don't let any of this discourage you, Matt. You've made good decisions up to this point. Don't doubt yourself now. Trust God to give you the strength to continue on the path He had set before you."

"But will that path include Laurel, Rose and the baby?" Matt asked. "After this morning, I'm not sure."

"What do you mean?"

"This week I've done a lot of thinking and praying. I had some Godly advice given to me by a friend, and last night I confronted my brother's anger without letting my own overpower me. I felt like I'd survived the test and was confident for the first time ever, that I could be a father to Rose and the baby. Then I got the call from Jessa about Laurel coming to the hospital." Matt rubbed a hand on his chest. "I was so scared that something would happen to her or the baby. Only when I got here, she wouldn't have anything to do with me. She thought I would be happy she might lose the baby. That I had been praying for this to happen." Matt looked at Dean. "I never prayed for that. Never."

"Laurel's going through a lot right now. I'm sure that given a little time, she'll come around."

"But I'm afraid if she loses the baby, she'll never believe me."

"Didn't they say that the ultrasound showed the baby was okay?" Dean reminded him.

"Yes, but there's obviously something still wrong with Laurel. And as long as there's something wrong with Laurel, the baby is at risk too."

Dean's gaze went passed Matt. "Looks like another doctor has shown up."

Matt rose from his chair, but then just stood there. "I guess I have to wait to see what Violet says. Laurel won't want me in the room. I just feel so...useless."

"I know Laurel may have said she doesn't want you in the room, but I'm guessing that just knowing you're out here has made an impact on her."

Matt sat back down, hoping what Dean had said was true. They were still waiting for news fifteen minutes later when Jessa showed up.

"How is Laurel?" she asked when she spotted them in the waiting area.

"Violet fired the doctor that was looking after her when he

wanted to send her home without figuring out what caused all the pain to start with. I think the new doctor is in with her and Violet now," Matt told her.

Jessa's brows drew together. "Why aren't you with her?"

Matt sighed. "She told me she didn't want me there. She thinks I'm happy that there is a chance she might lose the baby."

Jessa was quiet for a moment then said, "Let me go see what's happening."

"Now she's the one I would have expected to raise a ruckus over Laurel's care," Dean commented. "I guess Violet's got a little bit of Julia in her after all."

"All it takes is the right circumstances to bring out parts of a person they never knew existed...good and bad." Matt kept watching down the hall, hoping Jessa would return with some good news.

When she reappeared, she moved toward them with rapid strides. Both men stood as she approached.

❧ Chapter Fifteen ❧

THE other doctor didn't even wait for the blood work to come back," Jessa informed them, anger lacing her tone. "This new doctor has reviewed the results, and her white blood count is elevated. After doing a physical exam on her, he's thinking it may be her appendix. He reviewed the ultrasound that they did, but the technician focused entirely on the baby, so he's ordered another ultrasound to see if they can check the appendix that way. He's definitely not discharging her."

"If it's her appendix, what does that mean?" Matt asked.

"He'll have to do surgery to remove it," Jessa said.

"Surgery? But what about the baby?"

"The doctor said this is one of the most common surgeries performed on a woman during pregnancy. It isn't without risks, of course. The chance of Laurel miscarrying does go up, but there is still a really good chance she'll carry to term without any issues." Jessa held up her hands. "There is no other option. If her appendix is inflamed or has burst, surgery is a must."

Matt's stomach clenched. How he wished she'd let him be

with her. He wanted to hold her hand, kiss her forehead, and tell her everything was going to be okay. Instead, he was stuck out here because of his fears and inability to get over them sooner.

Jessa laid a hand on his arm. "I know you want to be in there with her. I asked her about it, but she refused to talk about you. Give her time. She is scared about losing the baby, and worried God isn't going to answer her prayers again." Then out of the blue, Jessa reached out to hug him. "Hang in there."

Once Jessa had returned to Laurel's room, Dean got a call and left to take care of sheriff business. He promised to come back as soon as he could and told Matt to call if he got any news. Left alone, Matt realized he should let Devon know what had happened. If nothing else, he knew Devon and his family would pray for them.

He had just finished talking on the phone when Violet appeared. She looked around the room. "Is Dean here?"

"He had to leave but said he'd be back later."

"Okay." She came and sat down next to him. "The ultrasound they just did showed her appendix is in fact inflamed and must come out. They are prepping her for surgery now."

"Can I see her?"

There was sadness on Violet's face as she shook her head. "I don't think that's a good idea. She does not even want to talk about you right now."

Though he nodded he understood, Matt wanted to be sick. Never had she rejected him outright like this. He just wanted a chance to tell her he loved her and wanted her and the baby to be fine.

"Once she goes to surgery, Jessa and I will come wait with you." And then, like her sister a short time before, Violet gave him a quick hug before heading back to Laurel's room.

Laurel watched the people moving around her. They were

arranging stuff in preparation for her surgery. She listened to explanation of what was to come, what might happen during the surgery and then she'd signed papers. The doctor assured her that the likelihood of something happening to her baby was slim, but none of it gave her any peace.

All she could think about was how she'd survive losing this baby after already losing her marriage. Because there was no way she could go back to Matt if she did lose their child. He hadn't wanted it, wouldn't consider a future with her as long as she'd carried it. Losing the baby would not make anything right between them. Matt could say he'd changed his mind about having kids, but it would all be empty words because the baby would be gone.

"Are you ready?" Jessa leaned over the side of the bed. She brushed back a strand of hair from Laurel's forehead. "We'll be waiting."

"Okay," Laurel said. "Thank you."

Violet also leaned over and gave her a kiss. "Love you, sis. See you in a bit."

They were both ushered out of the room, and then her bed was on the move. She stared up at the ceiling as the lights passed overhead. She counted them. Noticed where one bulb was missing. Through one set of doors. Then another. Voices surrounded her, but she tried her best to tune them out. She didn't want to think of what was to come and the ugly possibilities that lay ahead.

Everyone assured her that the odds of a successful surgery and pregnancy were in her favor, but until she held this baby in her arms, she wouldn't believe them. Of course, none of them knew what she'd given up to have this miracle in her life. There would be no going back to how things were before she'd found out she was pregnant, even if something did happen to the baby.

Once in the operating room they shifted her from the bed they'd wheeled her in on to the operating table. People were talking to her and asking her things, and she did her best to respond, but right then all she wanted to do was get this over with. Finally, they covered her mouth and nose with a mask, and everything faded away.

ॐ

"It's probably going to be about an hour before we hear anything," Jessa said. "I'm going to go find some coffee. You want something?"

"Sure," Matt replied. "Black coffee would be great."

"How about something to eat? I'm thinking you probably haven't eaten yet today."

"No, I haven't. I'm not picky though. Whatever is available would be great."

"I'm going to go with her," Violet said. "You okay on your own here? Or do you want to come with us?"

Matt shook his head. "I'm going to stick around here."

Once the women had left, Matt stood and walked to look out the large glass windows of the waiting room. He hadn't imagined that after coming to terms with his anger he wouldn't have a chance to tell Laurel about it. Now he wished he'd called her right away last night instead of waiting to tell her after he got off work. He'd planned to drive to Collingsworth after his work day was over to tell her in person. But now she didn't believe him, and he wasn't sure how to convince her otherwise, especially if something did happen to the baby.

"Matt?" He turned from the window to see the women had returned.

Violet set down a drink tray on the coffee table. Jessa also set down the cardboard container she carried and opened it up.

"Here," Violet handed him one of the Styrofoam cups with a lid on it. "And Jess got an assortment of donuts and muffins. Help yourself."

"Thanks," Matt said. He took a sip of the hot liquid, grateful that even in the hospital it was a decent cup of coffee. Though he wasn't really hungry, he went ahead and took a muffin. It didn't hold a candle to the ones Laurel made, but it would keep him going for a while.

Matt only half listened to the conversation between the two women. He couldn't keep his thoughts from Laurel and all she was going through. Everything he'd done had been out of love for her and his desire to protect her and this baby. Like they said, the road to hell was paved with good intentions. For sure his life would be a living hell if he and Laurel couldn't work this out. And he had no one to blame but himself.

Dean reappeared a short time later and after greeting Violet with a kiss, he came and sat down next to Matt.

"How you holding up? Violet called to update me on the situation."

"I'll be a lot better when she's out of surgery, and they come tell me she and the baby are going to be fine."

"I hear ya. I think I'd be a wreck if Violet was going through something like this."

"Show no weakness," Matt commented.

Dean shot him a look. "Something your dad used to say?"

Matt nodded. "I may look like I'm holding it together, but I'm a wreck inside. Even if she comes through all of this with flying colors, there's no guarantee she's going to give me a second chance. I have a feeling that because of my fear and stupidity I'm going to lose the best thing that's ever happened to me."

"I know all about doing stupid things when it comes to love. But Violet gave me a second chance, and I believe Laurel will give you one too. You've got her sisters on your side, so that's a big bonus. Just keep praying and trust that God will make this perfect in His time."

Matt nodded. He understood what Dean was saying, but he didn't want to wait. However now it was all in Laurel's hands. Somehow he needed to convince her that he'd never prayed she'd lose the baby, and that it hadn't made him happy or relieved to hear the pregnancy was in jeopardy.

Dean's phone rang, drawing his attention. When he finished talking, he gave Matt a rueful smile. "Going to have to run again."

Matt watched as he stood and walked over to Violet. She slipped her arm around his waist and lifted her face for his kiss. It reminded him of the intimacy he and Laurel had shared so often. He rubbed a hand on his chest as the ache there grew, taking away his breath. Would they ever share it again?

It wasn't long after Dean left that a doctor came into the waiting area. "Matt Davis?"

Matt stood and walked toward the man. "That's me."

"Your wife is out of surgery and in recovery now. Everything went perfectly. The appendix hadn't burst, so we were able to just remove it without any additional complications. The baby's heartbeat is strong and steady. A nurse will come and get you in a few minutes so you can go see her in the recovery room."

"Thank you, doctor," Matt said as he held out his hand to shake the doctor's.

"You're welcome. I'm just glad we caught it when we did." He turned to where Violet and Jessa stood. "I am sorry for the treatment you endured earlier today. There is no excuse for the delay in getting test results or the scans needed to diagnose her condition. The doctor will be dealt with."

"We appreciate your help with that and with Laurel," Jessa told him. "We didn't mean to cause waves, but when one of us is in trouble, we can't just sit back. Our grandmother taught us that."

The doctor smiled. "Yes, I can see you share that characteristic with her. She was a good woman."

Once the doctor had left Matt sank back down on his chair. He wasn't sure if he should be the one to go to the recovery room. She hadn't wanted to see him before; chances were she still wouldn't be thrilled to see him now.

"You should probably go," Matt told Violet when she

came to sit next to him. "I'm sure the surgery hasn't changed her mind about seeing me."

Violet didn't reply right away, but then slowly nodded. "Okay. I'll ask if she wants to see you and if so, I'll come get you right away."

"Thanks." Matt sighed. "I just want what's best for her. I want to be here for Laurel, but if she doesn't want me around, then I'll go."

Violet laid her hand on his arm. "Don't give up on her. We Collingsworth girls can be a little slow to figure things out, but it's worth it in the end."

"Oh, I know she's worth it. I will wait as long as she needs."

A nurse appeared and again asked for Matt. Violet and Jessa went and spoke to her and were soon led out of the waiting room. Matt watched them go then lowered his gaze to stare at the floor. He felt so helpless, and it was not a feeling he liked at all.

Trying to keep the negative emotions at bay, he pulled out his phone and sent a text message to Devon and his parents to update them on Laurel. Then he sat back to wait some more.

Violet and Jessa returned a short time later. Matt looked at Violet expectantly, but she gave him a small frown and shook her head. "She's in some pain, but they're giving her medication for that. Once she's a bit more comfortable they'll be bringing her back to her room."

"How long are they going to keep her in?" Matt asked.

"For at least tonight," Violet said. "They're going to monitor her and the baby for the next twenty-four hours. If everything looks okay and her pain is manageable, they'll send her home."

So now what did he do? Matt wondered. Did he hang around hoping Laurel would change her mind and see him? Did he head back to the Twin Cities? Or would they let him stay at the manor for the night?

"Matt, if you want to stay at the manor, you're more than welcome to," Jessa told him as if reading his mind.

"I'm not sure if that's the best thing. That's Laurel's home, and she's made it clear she doesn't want me around right now."

"She's not coming home until tomorrow most likely, so why don't you at least spend tonight," Violet suggested. "You look beat."

Matt nodded. "I am, so if you're sure..."

"We're sure," Jessa said. "Head over whenever you want. I think I'm going to hang around here until she's in her room, and I get a chance to see her. Then I'll be going home."

"I'll probably stay with her here for a while," Violet said. "I don't have anything pressing to do."

Matt wished he could say he'd stay with her too, but it wasn't his place any more apparently. "I think I'll wait until she's in her room as well, then I'll go and try to get a little sleep."

They didn't have to wait too long. Matt stood, but didn't follow the women as they headed down the hallway toward where a bed was being pushed into Laurel's room. Uncertain what to do, he sat back down, hoping one of them would come out soon and give him another update.

It was Jessa who reappeared and walked back to the waiting area. "She's doing good. The pain seems to be under control. I think she's really tired though. She didn't get much sleep last night, so it looks like she's going to sleep for a while. You want to head out to the manor now?"

Matt nodded. There was not much sense hanging around here right now. He walked with Jessa out to the parking lot and then followed her car to the manor. When he and Jessa walked into the house, Lily and Rose came flying to meet them.

"Is she okay?" Rose asked, her eyes wide with worry. Her gaze darted back and forth between Jessa and Matt.

"She's doing much better," Jessa assured her. "They had

to do surgery on her, but she and the baby are doing fine."

The relief was clear on Rose's face. "Can I see her?"

"She's sleeping now, but I'm going to go back up a little later. I'll take you with me," Jessa said.

Rose looked at Matt. She tilted her head to the side. "Why are you here?"

Trust a child to get right to the point. Obviously Laurel had told her about the state of their marriage. "Violet called to let me know what was happening to Laurel. I was worried about her so I came."

"She said you weren't together anymore."

"I'm hoping to change that," Matt told her. "I love her very much."

"Really?" Rose's face lit up. "So then you'd be my dad?"

Matt felt a rush of tears prick the backs of his eyes. As he looked down at the little girl in front of him, he wondered how he had ever thought he'd hurt her or the baby Laurel was carrying. "We'll have to see what Laurel says first."

"I hope she says yes. Then I'll have a mom, a baby brother or sister *and* a dad!"

Matt realized he now had one more person in favor of a reconciliation, and if anyone could convince Laurel to give him another chance, it just might be Rose. But he wondered if perhaps giving the little girl any kind of hope was a bad thing. In reality, he wanted Laurel to come back to him because she wanted to be with him, not because anyone convinced her it would be the right thing.

"The best thing you can do is pray," Matt told Rose.

"We need to give Laurel a little time to recover first," Jessa cautioned the little girl. "And right now Matt needs to get some sleep."

"Where do you want me to bunk down?" Matt asked.

"Go ahead and use Laurel's room," Jessa said. "I cleaned it up this morning, so everything is fresh."

"Thanks." Matt gripped the handle of his duffle bag and

climbed the stairs to the second floor. Once inside Laurel's room he leaned back against the door and let out a long sigh. With so much uncertainty right then, the oblivion of sleep seemed the most appealing. Maybe when he woke up some solutions would come to mind.

❧ *Chapter Sixteen* ❧

LAUREL shifted in the bed, biting her lip as a shaft of pain took her breath away. They had told her to let them know if she needed more pain medication, but she'd been trying to do without. Now the pain was bad, and it would probably take longer for it to take effect again.

"You okay, sweetie?" Violet leaned over her. "I can ask the nurses for pain meds if you need them."

"Yes, I think you'd better."

Violet rubbed her arm. "I'll be right back."

She was angry with herself for trying to be strong when she didn't need to be. More than anything she wanted this whole ordeal behind her. She wanted the pain to be gone. The baby to be fine. And to be able to get on with her life.

With or without Matt?

The thought caught her off guard. She'd been trying very hard not to think about Matt. But his face kept popping into her mind. Under different circumstances, he was the one she would have wanted by her side during all of this. Not that her sisters hadn't been great, but they weren't Matt.

Had he really changed? Or had he just said that for her benefit, so if she did lose the baby, she'd give them another chance? The pregnancy still wasn't out of the woods yet. She knew they were keeping a close eye on her and the baby, and so far things seemed okay, but that didn't take away the fear that things could change at any moment.

Violet returned with the nurse in tow. She carried a small tray with a cup of water and a white paper container.

"How are you feeling, dear?" the nurse asked as she checked the blood pressure monitor and the IV. "Do you think you could get up and walk a bit?"

The thought of walking made Laurel cringe, but she knew it was necessary. "Could I take something for the pain and let it take effect first?"

"Sure thing." The nurse handed her the water and paper cup containing the pills. "I'll come back in about thirty minutes to see how you're doing."

After Laurel took the medication, the nurse left the room. Violet settled back down on the chair next to the bed.

"You don't need to stay with me," Laurel told her. "I feel bad that you've been tied up here since early this morning. You need to sleep."

"I'm doing okay. Jessa is coming back up a little later. I'll probably go home then and try to get a quick nap."

"Thank you. I don't know what I would have done without you."

"I'm glad I can be here for you. Wouldn't want to be anywhere else," Violet assured her with a smile.

As she lay there, Laurel wished she was further along in her pregnancy so she could feel the baby's movements. It would be so much more reassuring. She laid her hand on her abdomen, careful to avoid the small incisions that had been made to remove her appendix. They had warned there might be more bleeding, but so far other than some really light spotting, it hadn't gotten any worse.

Far too soon, the nurse was back. "Ready to try walking?"

Laurel moved a bit, testing for pain. It was still there, but not as bad as it had been earlier. "Sure."

The nurse and Violet helped her into a sitting position. The movement brought on more pain, but once she was sitting it eased. Getting to her feet was easier and though she wanted to hunch over, the nurse urged her to stand straight. Before they left the room, the nurse gave her a robe to cover the back of the gown she wore.

"Don't want to flash the world, dear," she said with a grin.

Once out of the room, they turned to the right and headed in the direction of the nursing station. It was slow going, but Laurel found the more she moved, the better she felt. She was still grateful to have Violet there to lean on even as her other hand gripped the IV pole. It gave her hope that she was on the mend.

As they started back in the other direction, Laurel looked up and saw a couple of people walking toward them. She smiled as she recognized Rose and Jessa.

Rose waved and began to run to her. She must have been cautioned about hugging her though, because she stopped just short of throwing her arms around Laurel. Instead she stood close and lifted her head, a big smile on her face.

"Hi, sweetheart," Laurel said as she reached out to brush a lock of blond hair from Rose's cheek. "How are you doing?"

"I'm fine. How are you?"

"I'm doing better. Especially since you're here now."

Rose's brow furrowed. "Is the baby okay?"

"So far, the baby is fine. We just have to keep praying it stays that way."

"Why don't we go back into the room," Violet suggested.

Laurel slipped the arm without the IV around Rose's shoulders. They walked into the hospital room and the nurse helped Laurel get settled in the bed again. Jessa set the vase of flowers she'd been carrying on the table next to the bed.

"They're beautiful. Thank you."

Jessa smiled. "I'll pass it on."

"What?" Laurel asked.

"They're from Matt."

When Laurel turned to look at them again, she realized she should have known that right away. They were the flowers Matt would always bring her just because. When they were dating, he'd asked her what type of flower she liked. She'd told him roses—one of every color. And ever since then he'd brought her bouquets of roses in an assortment of colors. No two were ever the same. He probably now understood the significance of the rose to Laurel.

She wanted to cry looking at them. She had her real Rose now, but had lost everything else. "Is he still in town?"

Jessa and Violet exchanged glances before Jessa nodded. "He went back to the manor to get some sleep, but he's in the waiting room now. Did you want to talk to him?"

Laurel looked again at the flowers. The anger she'd felt when she'd seen Matt that first time still lingered, mixed in with fear. She wanted to say yes, but she wasn't sure if she was up to the frank and honest discussion they needed to have. And she didn't think the hospital was the place to have it.

"Not right now. Let me spend some time with Rose first."

Violet nodded. "I'll take her home with me when you're done visiting. Jessa said she'd stay with you this evening."

"You guys don't have to put everything on hold for me."

"Don't worry about it," Jessa said as she patted her hand. "This is what family is for."

"Why don't we leave you and Rose for a bit?" Violet suggested.

"Sure. I'd like that," Laurel said. After Jessa and Violet had left, Rose sat down on the chair Violet had been occupying.

"Do you like to color?" she asked.

"Color?" Laurel watched as Rose dug into a bag she'd

brought with her.

"Yes. I love to color." She set two coloring books on the bed and then pulled out a large worn box of crayons. "Some say it's for babies, but I think it's fun."

"That sounds like something my speed right now," Laurel agreed.

Rose held up the two coloring books. "Which one do you want?"

"Why don't you pick the picture you'd like me to color? I think you're better at this than I am."

Rose nodded and bent her head as she paged through the first book. Laurel could see a lot of the pictures were already colored, but finally the little girl stopped on one page and handed the book to her. This coloring book wasn't what she was expecting. The page Rose had chosen for her was an intricate picture of a fairy in a garden, not at all like the Barbie doll pictures she used to color as a child. A quick flip through the other pictures showed her that Rose took her coloring seriously.

"These are beautiful, sweetheart! Are you sure you want me to color one? I don't think I'll do as good a job as you."

"Just do your best," Rose said with a grin.

Laurel wanted to laugh, but decided it would hurt too much so just returned her daughter's smile. "I will certainly do that."

Rose helped Laurel get the wheeled table up to the bed so she could use that to color on, and then settled cross-legged back in the chair. She had a clipboard that she used to support her coloring book. After much consideration, she chose her first color and then handed the box to Laurel.

Laurel was surprised at how much she actually enjoyed the coloring. Rose chattered on about friends and even though school was out, she talked about her teachers and the classes she'd had the previous year. Laurel figured she learned more about her daughter in that half hour than she had in all the years up to that point.

"How are you two doing?" Jessa's voice had them both looking toward the doorway. "I see she got you to do some coloring with her."

"Yes, and I'm really enjoying it," Laurel told her with a smile.

"I'm glad to hear it because Rose loves to color." Jessa smiled at the young girl. "Are you about ready to head home with Violet?"

Rose's shoulders slumped, but she nodded. "I guess so."

"Maybe Violet can bring you back up after supper, okay?"

Rose nodded as she began to pack up the crayons and coloring books. "Thanks for coloring with me."

"Thanks for letting me," Laurel replied. "I really enjoyed it."

Beaming, Rose left the room with Jessa. Laurel knew what was coming and tried to quell the butterflies in her stomach. She didn't know if she was ready for this, but she couldn't avoid Matt forever.

A few minutes after she left with Rose, Jessa reappeared. "Violet's taken her home. Are you up to talking with Matt now?"

"I suppose."

"We're not trying to force the issue, if you're really not feeling up to it. He said he'd wait."

"No, I think we need to talk."

"Okay. I'm going to run over to the shop. Text me when you and Matt are finished talking. If you need me to come back." Jessa bent over and kissed her cheek. "I'll be praying for you guys. Keep your heart open."

"I'll try," Laurel said.

Once Jessa had left, Laurel was suddenly aware of how she must look. She ran her hands over her hair, dismayed to find it flat and matted in spots, but there was nothing she could do now.

She rested back against the pillows, glad the bed had been

raised to a position that allowed her to semi-recline without having to lay flat on her back. Sitting without the support hurt her abdomen a bit more than she wanted.

A knock drew her attention, and she saw Matt standing in the doorway. As she looked at him, she realized how much she'd missed this man. But there was still so much between them that made her nervous to be around him.

"Come in," she said with a wave of her hand.

He moved to the side of the bed and sat down on the chair most recently occupied by her daughter. "Did you have a good visit with Rose?"

Laurel nodded and told him about coloring with her. "She's definitely got an artistic streak in her that she didn't get from me."

Matt tilted his head. "You never did say who her father was."

"He was a boy whose dad had come to teach at the college for a semester."

"Did he know you were pregnant?"

Laurel shook her head. "By the time I found out, they had moved on. We ended things before he left, since we knew it couldn't go anywhere."

"Had you tried to track him down since then? To tell him he has a daughter?"

"No. And I don't plan to. If Rose decides one day she wants to find him, I'll give her the information I have about him, but right now he would be a complication I don't need."

Matt seemed to contemplate that for a moment, and then nodded. "She asked me if I was going to be her dad."

Laurel swallowed hard. "What did you tell her?"

"That we would have to see how things worked out."

Laurel plucked at the sheet covering her legs. "I don't understand what's happened with you. One day you're set on never having children, and then when it appears I'm losing the baby, you show up here and say you've changed your mind."

"I know it seems sudden, and as if it is tied to what happened with you, but the reality is, I had planned to come up today after work to talk to you again."

"About changing your mind?"

"I'm not sure it's so much about changing my mind, but seeing things from a different perspective. Devon came to see me after you called him."

Laurel winced. "Sorry if you felt I sicced him on you. I didn't mean for him to go and try to convince you to change your mind. I just didn't want you to be alone."

Matt gave her a small smile. "I'm not upset with you. It turned out to be a good thing."

"I'll be honest, I can't reconcile all I've learned about you in the past week with the man I've been married to for the past two years. I can't decide if I've been married to a fake or a changed man."

"I'd like to think I'm a changed man. That's one of the things Devon helped me see. The anger and the fighting...it was all part of who I was before I became a Christian."

Laurel nodded slowly. "That would make more sense."

Matt leaned forward, resting his elbows on his knees. "Listen, I know the timing seems off. I know you're not certain I'm here for the long haul because I showed up when you thought your pregnancy was in jeopardy."

Laurel sighed. "I'm very confused. I want to believe you, but I'm still trying to come to grips with everything I've learned about you this past week. Everything is just so confusing right now."

Matt straightened in his seat, his face emotionless. "If you had known all that when we first started dating, would you have considered marrying me?"

Laurel mulled over his question. Would she have married him if she'd known about what he'd done as a child and then later as a teenager?

"I wanted to put that part of my life behind me. I figured

the best way to do that was just not tell you about it, and then make sure my worst fears would never be realized by getting you to agree to not having children," Matt said. "Of course, I didn't know you already had a daughter."

"I don't know how I would have reacted," Laurel said honestly. "I would like to think I would have had an open mind."

Matt's gaze dropped away from hers as he lowered his head. "I've had precious few good things in my life. The first was Devon and his family, and then you came along. You were beautiful, gentle and kind, all the things that hadn't been part of my life. I was just too selfish. I didn't want to take the chance of losing you. Of course, in the end, that's what has happened anyway, so I guess I could have saved us both a lot of heart ache if I'd just been upfront about it all."

Laurel's heart clenched at his words, and the anger lessened just a bit. "Is there other stuff I should know? Is it just you and your brother or do you had other siblings?"

Matt looked up. "Just us. And my mother, whom I haven't seen since the night I killed my dad."

"Why didn't you see her after that?"

"She denied my dad had beaten us. I found out later she tried to say I was the one with the anger issue, and I had killed my dad while in a rage. Thankfully no one believed her, or I would have been dealt with in a much different way." Matt sighed. "My mother must have been a few sandwiches short of a picnic to think the cops wouldn't see the bruises all over her, Steven and me. I don't know if she's still in contact with Steven or not."

"Speaking of bruises...your face?" Laurel asked.

Matt touched his forehead. "Yeah, this just happened last night." Once again, Matt recounted what had happened the night before. "By the time he jumped me, the cops were already on their way."

"How does he look?"

"He's not sporting any wounds from my hands. I

defended myself, but didn't fight back. I looked at it as a test. The other night at the hospital I did punch him, but believe me, it was nothing compared to what I wanted to do to him. I didn't see it that night, but already then I was controlling my reaction. I wanted to do a lot more damage to Steven to try to knock some sense into him, but my own common sense prevailed. Last night I managed to keep my head clear and didn't even try to punch him. I think he got roughed up a bit from the cops, but only because he kept resisting arrest."

"It sounds like he has more of an anger issue than you do."

Matt nodded. "Yes, he's like I was as a teen. Last night I realized maybe Devon was right, that I had changed since becoming a Christian."

"And that's why you've changed your mind about having children?" Laurel asked.

He didn't say anything right away, but then Matt slowly nodded. He looked at Laurel and said, "My reason for not wanting kids has nothing to do with not liking them. It's because I think children are special that I didn't want to have any. I didn't ever want to be responsible for hurting one."

"And you don't think you'll hurt Rose or this baby?"

✌ *Chapter Seventeen* ✌

MATT'S brow furrowed. "I'm still scared, Laurel. My heart wants to believe I can do this. That I can take on fatherhood without experiencing any sort of anger issues. I guess what I want is a chance. You know everything now; I want us to deal with all that's to come together."

Laurel's first instinct was still to protect Rose and the baby. If there was even a chance Matt might hurt them, as much as she loved Matt she wouldn't put her children in danger. "Are you willing to go to counselling?"

"If that's what you need me to do," Matt said. "I'll do whatever you want me to do to put your mind at ease. Which, in turn, will put my own mind at ease."

There was still a hesitation in Laurel's heart, and she couldn't figure out if it was there because of her own fear or if it was God's way of cautioning her. "I believe you want this to work, that you think you can handle things now. I just want to take it slow. We've got six months or so before the baby comes, so we've got time to work through things, to see if you really do have a handle on this."

Matt nodded. "Just give this a chance, that's all I ask. If

you ever feel threatened by me or feel Rose isn't safe, leave. I will always expect you to put your and the children's safety above me. I would insist on it."

"I guess we'll be apart this next month, regardless," Laurel said.

"Yes, for part of it. I'm going to ask my supervisor for at least one week off even though it is our busy time of year, and I'll also try to make it up every weekend."

Laurel laid a hand on her stomach. "I'm not going to be much help with the renovations with all that's happened."

"I'll help pick up the slack when I'm around, though honestly, I'm not sure your gran really expected you girls to actually do the work. I think she just wanted to get you all together to try to repair the relationships now that she's gone."

"You're probably right," Laurel agreed.

They lapsed into silence for a minute before Laurel pushed herself to a sitting position.

Matt stood, concern on his face. "Take it easy."

"Tell that to my bladder," Laurel said as she eased her legs over the side of the bed.

"Ah." Matt held out his hand. "Let me help you."

Without speaking, Laurel put her hand into his and gripped it tightly as she slid to a standing position. Once on her feet, she stood still for a minute. When she began to take hesitant steps, her hand gripping the IV pole, he moved with her until they got to the door of the bathroom.

"You okay to take it from here?" Matt asked.

Laurel nodded. "But I'm not going to lock the door."

As she finished up in the bathroom, Laurel heard Jessa's voice and was relieved to hear her say something about getting more pain meds for her. Laurel opened the door to find Matt still there waiting for her. He held out his hand again, and she took it without hesitation. She was getting settled back into bed when Jessa reappeared.

"Hey, sweetie," Jessa said as she approached the bed. "Matt said maybe you needed more pain meds?"

Laurel nodded. "The soreness is becoming more than just sore."

"The nurse will bring you something in a minute. I phoned earlier and asked what you could eat." She gestured to the bag on the table. "They said soup or soft foods, so I went to the café and had Elsa put some food together for us."

As Jessa unpacked the containers and set them on the table, the nurse came in with the pain meds.

"Smells lovely in here," she commented as she handed the pills and water to Laurel. "Supper?"

"Yep," Jessa said. "But nothing too fancy for the patient. Just some cream of potato cheddar soup."

"That sounds about right for her," the nurse agreed. "Hopefully tomorrow she'll be back to more normal food, but don't go hog wild with a steak or the like. Slowly build back up to foods like that. Allow your system to settle back down again."

After the nurse left, Jessa handed Matt a bowl of soup and a sandwich. "Wasn't sure exactly what you liked, but figured most men like roast beef. I had Elsa put everything on the side so you can add what you want to it."

"Thanks. I'm starving."

❧

Matt was pleased to see Laurel make a dent in her soup. After finishing his own food, he polished off Laurel's when she decided she was full. They had just cleaned up the food containers when Violet and Dean showed up with Lily and Rose in tow. Thankfully because of the private room Laurel was in, they were allowed more visitors in the room as long as Laurel was up to it.

Lily didn't stay long before heading off to meet up with some friends, and Dean and Violet left shortly after. Jessa said she was going to visit her best friend for about an hour and would come back to pick up Rose. When it was just the three of them, Rose pulled out her coloring books again. There wasn't room for all three of them to color, so Rose sat up on the bed with Laurel. Matt sat in the chair, legs stretched out and watched them. The two blonde heads bent close together as they colored and chatted.

He could see now that Laurel was a natural mother. Her tender and caring nature had been what had drawn him to her in the first place. Matt knew now it had been wrong of him to ask her to agree to never having children. Even though she had agreed, he should never have even asked that of her. In asking Laurel not to have children, he'd been no better than her grandmother who had taken Rose from her. He just wished he had some assurance he'd be as good a father as she was a mother.

The hour passed quickly, and it wasn't long before Jessa was back to collect Rose. Matt could see neither was happy about the separation, but it was necessary for at least one more night.

"You don't have to stay," Laurel said once they were alone.

"I have nowhere else to be," Matt told her. "Unless you want me to leave."

Laurel shook her head. "No, not at all. But I think I'm going to probably fall asleep pretty quick here. The pain meds have helped, and my tummy is full. I just hope I don't have a bad bout of morning sickness tomorrow. That is going to hurt."

"Is it still pretty bad?" Matt asked.

"It's eased up a bit. It's not every single morning now. I'm almost done the first trimester, so it's supposed to get better."

"Do you feel up to a little walk before you sleep? I know the nurse was encouraging you to move around."

Laurel nodded. "I know I need to be moving more."

Walking with a little more confidence, Laurel left the room holding tightly to Matt's arm. They made a couple of trips up and down the hallway before Laurel was ready to return to her room. She made one last trip to the bathroom before crawling back into her bed. Matt helped her get settled, reclining the bed a bit more. Once she was comfortable, he sat back down in the chair, prepared to wait until she'd drifted off before leaving.

"Did Devon tell you that Amy is pregnant?" Matt asked her.

Laurel lay on her side facing him, her hand curled up under the pillow. Her eyes widened. "No, he didn't mention that."

"I don't think they've told many people as she's not far along, but I think he wanted me to know I wouldn't be alone on this journey to fatherhood."

"I'm happy for them, and it will be nice to have friends who have a little one almost the same age."

Matt could see she was fighting to keep her eyes open, so he didn't continue the conversation and pretty soon he could tell she was asleep. In no rush to get back to the manor, Matt stayed at her bedside for a while longer. A nurse came in to check on her, smiling when she saw him sitting there.

"I think she's probably out for a few hours now," she said in a low voice.

"Yes, I hope so. I just wanted to make sure before I go." Pulling his legs in, Matt stood. "Can you tell her its fine for her to call me if she wakes in the night and wants to talk?"

A wide smile stretched across the nurse's face. "Will do. Hopefully she'll be able to go home with you tomorrow. As long as she's not in too much pain, her blood pressure is okay and the baby is doing well, she should be good to go."

"We'll be glad to have her home, that's for sure." After pressing a soft kiss to Laurel's cheek, Matt said goodnight to the nurse and left the room.

It was still light when he left the hospital. The summer days meant daylight lingered until after nine each night. In past years they had enjoyed the longer days, going for walks or sitting in their back yard on the swing talking. He hoped it wouldn't be long before they were able to do that yet again.

Matt woke the next morning and reached immediately for his phone to see if he'd missed a text from Laurel. There were no alerts on the screen, so he laid back against his pillow. He wondered what the day ahead held. It was hard to believe it was only Saturday, just barely twenty-four hours since he'd gotten the phone call from Jessa. He hoped the doctors released Laurel from the hospital, but only if it really was safe for her to come back to the manor.

He needed to make a decision about what he was going to do next week. A lot depended on what Laurel wanted. Though he wanted to be here with her, if she felt she needed space, he would respect her wishes.

He thought about the men's retreat and the speaker's challenge to give each day to God and trust Him for the outcome that would glorify and honor Him the most. Devon had also encouraged him each day to claim the promise from the Bible that if any man is in Christ, he is a new creation. So before getting out of bed, Matt closed his eyes and prayed.

"Heavenly Father, thank you for a new day. A day of hope and promise. I ask that You guide me through this day, that my words and actions will glorify You. Help me to trust You regardless of what may unfold. And help me to be the new creation You have made me to be. I can't overcome the chains of my past without Your help. I want my life, my marriage and my role as father to be glorifying to You. I commit all of this into Your hands for Your glory. Amen."

Feeling a bit more hopeful about the day that lay ahead, Matt got out of bed and headed to the bathroom for a shower and to get ready to go to the hospital. Downstairs a little while later, he found Jessa and Violet in the kitchen. The smell of coffee was heavy in the air, and he breathed in deeply.

Violet grinned at him. "Would you like an actual cup of the stuff?"

"Oh yes," Matt said. "Can't start my day without it."

"Do you want something to eat?" Jessa asked. "We've got a variety of cereals. Bread for toast. Eggs if you're up for making yourself some."

"I'll just have some cereal and toast," Matt said. "Point me in the direction, and I'll get it for myself."

"I can put the toast in," Jessa said as she pointed to the pantry. "The cereal is in there."

Violet set a cup of coffee on the table and then settled down in a chair with her own. "Do you think they're going to let Laurel out today?"

Matt took the bowl Jessa held out. "I sure hope so, but only if she's ready."

"How are things between the two of you?" Jessa put two pieces of toast on a plate and brought it to the table.

"I think they're better." Matt poured milk on his cereal and then sat down. "But it's really hard to know for sure with Laurel. It's been difficult for us both. Our hearts have wanted one thing, but logic dictated another."

"And that's changed?" Jessa set some jam and peanut butter on the table along with a knife. "Are you willing to be a father now?"

"Yes. I am. I was able to talk with a friend who gave me some good insight." Matt took a spoonful of cereal and ate it. "I know now I should never have hidden my past from her. I know she had her own reasons for thinking not having kids would be okay, but if we'd both been upfront about our past, it would have been better. Secrets are just not the way to go."

"I agree with you there, but it seems to run in the family," Violet said. "Gran, rest her soul, was a big one for secrets. I still don't think we've uncovered all she kept. We might not ever know them all."

"I still think you're exaggerating," Jessa said.

"One word. William." Violet took another sip of her coffee.

Jessa frowned. "Okay, that was a big secret. But I can't

believe there's more."

"I can. We still don't know anything about Mama, and I believe Gran knew before she died where Mama was, or at least what happened to her."

Matt sensed tension between the sisters when Violet mentioned their mother. Not wanting to get into the middle of it, he focused on finishing their breakfast. Neither of them said anything more either, so an awkward silence filled the room. After he drained the last of his coffee, Matt stood and took his dishes to the sink.

"Just leave those there, Matt," Jessa said. "I'll put them in the dishwasher with the rest."

"Thank you. I'm going to head up to the hospital now. I'll let you know as soon as we hear what's going on with Laurel."

"Sounds good," Violet said. "I hope it's good news."

"Me, too."

"You might want to take her some fresh clothes if there's a chance they'll discharge her today," Violet suggested. "I don't think she wants to wear home what she wore when I took her into the hospital."

"Good idea. I didn't even think about that."

"That's what we sisters are here for," Violet said with a smile.

After packing a small bag with some clothes and toiletries for Laurel, Matt stepped out the front door into a bright, warm morning. He didn't linger to enjoy it though. Within minutes he was turning from the driveway onto the road that led to Collingsworth. He was glad it was such a quick drive to the hospital.

When he got up to Laurel's room, there were a few people in the room with her. He hesitated in the doorway, uncertain about whether he should go in or not. Laurel happened to look his way and when she saw him, she waved him in.

The people in the room made room for him to approach the side of Laurel's bed.

"Everything okay?" Matt looked from Laurel to the doctor he recognized from the day before who had done her surgery.

"So far everything looks good for your wife. We're going to do another ultrasound to check on the baby before we make the decision to discharge her. If everything looks okay, then I think she should be able to go home. Hopefully by noon we'll know for sure which way things are going to go."

The doctor and the four other people he had with him left the room. As Matt sat down on the chair he noticed she no longer had the IV in her arm and figured that was a good sign. "How are you feeling?"

She smiled slightly. "Much better than yesterday. And the pain is manageable. I will just need to take it easy for a while."

"I think that can be arranged," Matt assured her. He lifted the bag he'd packed. "Violet told me you might want a few things. Hope I packed the right stuff."

Laurel patted the bed beside her. "Let me see."

Matt set the bag down so she could open it. She looked through the contents quickly and then glanced up with a smile. "You did good. I think there is everything I need to at least look passable if they let me go."

"Did you have breakfast already?"

Laurel nodded. "I asked for oatmeal, and they let me have it. The nurse even helped me with a shower so I could wash my hair."

"Did you sleep okay?" Matt sat down and leaned back in the chair, linking his hands over his abdomen.

"I was surprised that I actually slept pretty well. I woke up once and had some more pain meds, but then slept through until morning." She swung her feet over the edge of the bed. "Want to walk? I know they are after me to do some more walking still."

Matt stood and held out his elbow so that she could slip her hand into the crook of his arm. He kept his steps slow as they left the room and moved down the hallway. It was quickly apparent that she was moving a lot better than the night before. The nurses at the station offered words of encouragement as they walked past them.

They had planned to do another lap, but a nurse stopped them to say the ultrasound had been arranged. Matt tried to keep his nervousness from showing. Now that he had accepted the idea of becoming a father, the thought of losing the baby was unbearable. But if that should happen, he wouldn't try to prevent Laurel from getting pregnant again. Given what they'd gone through though, it seemed so important that this little one survive.

⨭ Chapter Eighteen ⨴

*L*AUREL seemed calmer than he was as they prepped her for the ultrasound. Matt sat on the chair next to the bed where he could see the monitor as well. He reached for her hand and held it as the technician lifted her gown and squirted gel onto her lower abdomen.

"I realize you're a little tender. Just let me know if I'm pressing too hard," she said as she picked up the scanner.

At first the woman didn't say anything. She just moved the scanner around, pressing buttons on the machine as she did. Finally she turned and smiled at them. "I'll have the doctor review the results, but I'll show you this."

She moved the scanner into position again, and the side profile of a tiny baby came into focus. Then she pointed to the screen. "That's your baby's heart beating. It's an active little one. Lots of moving around."

Matt swallowed hard as he stared at the little life that was safely contained in Laurel's womb. It was so unbelievable. That the small figure was a part of him and the woman he loved so much.

"And here, have a listen." The technician turned another knob, and suddenly a rapid beating sound filled the room. "Your baby's heartbeat."

Matt worked to keep his emotions under control. To have this good news after going through so much over the past few weeks was almost unreal.

The woman punched a few more buttons and then tore off a strip of paper. She handed it to Laurel. "Here are some pictures of your little one."

Laurel looked at them, then let go of Matt's hand to touch the paper with a fingertip. A small smile played around her lips. She looked at Matt as she handed him the paper. The images were the same as what they'd seen on the screen, but now it seemed even more real to hold a picture in his hand.

Once it was just the two of them in Laurel's room, Matt said, "That was pretty amazing."

"Yes," Laurel agreed, her voice soft. "I had basically prepared myself for the worst, so to see the baby so active and with such a strong heartbeat... I'm very grateful."

Before Matt could say anything more, the doctor came into the room. This time he was on his own.

He stood at the foot of Laurel's bed and smiled at them. "It looks like you're good to go. The ultrasound showed that the baby is doing fine. Of course, we will give you instructions on things to watch out for once you're home. And you'll need to make an appointment with your own doctor for two weeks."

"Thank you for everything," Laurel said.

"It was my pleasure," the doctor replied. "A positive outcome is always what we strive for, so I'm glad we were able to have that in your case. I'll have the nurse come in with the discharge papers and instructions for the care of your incisions. If you had any questions, please don't hesitate to ask."

Within the hour, Laurel was in a wheelchair, and they were on their way out of the hospital. Though he would have liked for them to be returning to their own home, Matt was glad he would have the help of Laurel's sisters to keep her from doing too much. If they were at their house, she'd be trying to cook and clean when she needed to be resting. At the manor, he knew Jessa and Violet would make sure she took it easy.

"Guess I should have brought your car," Matt said as he opened the passenger door of his truck. "It would be easier to get in and out of."

"This is fine," she told him. "They say I'm supposed to be moving around more. Walking. Going up and down stairs. Do don't worry about it."

"It's my job to worry about you." Matt held the seatbelt out so that she could snap it in. "Let's get you home."

Realizing he'd forgotten to let Violet and Jessa know what was going on, he told her she might want to give one of them a call. She found her phone in her purse and discovered it was dead.

"Just use mine," Matt said and handed it to her.

As he drove, he listened as she talked to one of them, telling them about all that had transpired that morning. "We're almost there. I'll tell you the rest when we arrive."

She handed the phone back to him. "I'll be glad to be back at the manor. It seems like I've been away much longer than just a day though."

"Not much has changed." Matt paused and then said, "Um, Jessa told me to stay in your room last night. I'll move my stuff to another room when we get there."

He glanced at her hoping she'd shake her head, but instead she said, "That might be best for now."

Matt's throat was too tight for him to talk, so he just nodded. They didn't say anything more as he turned into the driveway to the manor. When he pulled the truck to a stop, Rose burst out the front door and ran toward them. Matt got out and rounded the truck to help Laurel out.

"Be gentle with her, sweetheart," Matt told Rose before he opened the door. "Her tummy is still sore."

Rose looked up at him and nodded. When Laurel slid out of the truck, Rose gently put her arms around her mother's waist. Laurel wrapped Rose in a hug and pressed a kiss to her hair. "Missed you, sweetie."

"I missed you too. I'm so glad you're home."

Matt carried the things she'd had at the hospital into the house. "Do you want to go lay down?"

Laurel shook her head. "I've been laying down a lot. I'd like to just sit down here for a bit."

"Okay. I'll take your stuff up to your room." Once up there, he put the few things he'd pulled out that morning back into his duffle bag. He had just stepped from the room when Jessa appeared out of a door down the hallway.

"Laurel mentioned you moving to a different room tonight," Jessa said and motioned to the room she'd just left. "This is Cami's room, but you can use it since she's not around. There are clean sheets on the bed."

"Thanks." Matt was grateful that she didn't ask any questions and was just matter of fact about it. He dropped his bag onto the floor as he sat down on the edge of the bed. He still wasn't sure what he should do about going back to the Twin Cities. Having made a few tentative steps forward, Matt was reluctant to leave Laurel. He didn't want to lose any ground they'd gained in the past twelve hours.

When he got back down to the kitchen, he found all the sisters together. They seemed to be discussing the upcoming renovations.

"We're going to need to go through Gran's room," Violet said.

"You haven't done anything with it yet?" Laurel asked.

Jessa shook her head. "I just haven't wanted to deal with all of that. But I guess we'd better get that storage bin like Lance suggested so we can store her stuff in there until we decide what to do with it."

"Hey, Matt," Rose said when she saw him. The others looked to where he stood in the kitchen entrance.

"Hope I'm not interrupting," he said as he came further into the room.

"Not at all," Violet assured him. "Just trying to sort through some logistics for the upcoming renovations."

Matt settled onto a stool at the counter and listened as they continued to figure out their next course of action to prepare for having their lives disrupted for a stretch of time.

It wasn't too long before Laurel began to fade, so, after taking some meds, she retreated back upstairs to her room. Matt would have liked to join her, but instead he took his phone and walked out behind the house to the shore. He settled onto the wooden swing and made a call to his boss. After talking with him, he decided that he would take Monday off too, but if everything went okay with Laurel, he'd be back on Tuesday.

He really didn't want to leave, but he knew Laurel wanted to take things slow. His being in a separate bedroom was proof of that. So he'd leave for a few days and then make his way back on the weekend. His conditions on their relationship were what had gotten them in this mess, so he was willing to let her call the shots now until she was comfortable with how things were with them. Now he needed to pray to God for more patience.

After talking to his boss, Matt called Devon to give him an update.

"That's certainly an answer to prayer," Devon said after Matt told him what had transpired that morning. "We'll continue to pray about your relationship with Laurel. I think it will be fine, maybe even better than it was now that there are no more secrets between you."

"I hope you're right. She seems to want space right now. It's hard to give that to her, but really, it's the least I can do after everything else wrong I've done."

"Patience, my friend," Devon told him. "Just remind yourself how worth it she is."

"Yes, she definitely is."

After talking a bit longer, Matt ended the call. He didn't go back to the house right away. The peace and quiet of the lake soothed his soul. Looking at the beauty around him, he was reminded that God was the one who had created all of this. His handiwork was truly a beautiful thing. Matt had to believe that their marriage was also His handiwork and in time would be as beautiful as God's other creations.

☙❧

Laurel slept a couple of hours and woke feeling even better. It seemed that each time she slept, her body recovered a bit more. She hoped it wouldn't be long until she felt like her old self again. Downstairs she found Violet and Rose in the kitchen, but there was no sign of Jessa, Matt or Lily.

"Lily is with Nate and some of their friends," Violet told her. "I think Matt is at the greenhouse with Jessa. She had some building ideas she wanted to ask him about."

Laurel settled onto one of the stools at the counter. "Are you making supper?"

"I guess you could call it that." Violet grinned. "Just frying some ground beef to go with the store bought tortilla shells."

"Sounds good to me. Want me to cut up anything for you?" Laurel asked. "I think I can safely do that from a sitting position."

As Violet cooked up the meat, Laurel took care of chopping the tomatoes, onions and lettuce. Rose even pitched in and carefully grated the cheese. Laurel had just finished the lettuce when the back door opened. She saw Matt standing there holding it open for Jessa. Her heart skipped a beat at the sight of him.

How she hoped that he really had changed and that they had a future together. Now it was more than just him accepting the baby and Rose. He needed to show that he could control his anger. Part of her felt it wouldn't be a problem. After all, hadn't they been together over three years now with him not showing any more anger or frustration than the average person? At least when she'd been around. But she suspected that if he'd gotten into fights at work, he wouldn't still have a job there. However, knowing what she did about his past, there was now a little doubt and fear in her heart. If Rose and the baby weren't in the picture, she wouldn't be as worried because she could take care of herself. She needed some sort of peace before she could fully commit to getting back together with Matt.

Supper ended up being a somewhat chaotic affair. Dean and Addy showed up and accepted the invitation to stay. Then Lily and Nate appeared as they were dishing up. Thankfully there was plenty of food, and people just snagged a chair wherever they could find one. Laurel enjoyed being surrounded by her family and with Matt and Rose both there, for the first time, Collingsworth felt more like home for her than it ever had.

But she was still feeling the effects of the past few days and called it a night before everyone had left. Matt walked her up to the room.

"You need any help?" he asked.

"No, I'm fine. The pain's not too bad, I'm just really tired."

"Okay." He gave her a smile that didn't quite reach his eyes. "I'll see you in the morning."

Laurel nodded then watched as he left the room, closing the door behind him. It was an odd feeling to think of him sleeping somewhere else in the house beside her bed, but she didn't want to get distracted by his presence. She didn't want her desire for closeness to him to override her need for peace in her heart.

Laurel woke during the night, and it took a moment for her to realize where she was. So much had transpired in the past forty-eight hours it almost felt like a dream. But she was glad to be back in her own bed without being attached to machines and an IV. The ache in her abdomen had returned, and she needed to go to the bathroom. Moving slowly, she got up and went to take her pain medication. She had learned now to go ahead and take it before the pain worsened or it just took that much longer to take effect.

Once she had the medication and was settled back into bed, Laurel closed her eyes in hopes of falling back asleep, but instead, she found her thoughts drifting. Safe in the quiet of her room, she could finally allow herself to really think and pray over all that had transpired. She was struggling to trust God completely with everything. And she realized that even though she'd prayed for Matt to change his mind, she really hadn't believed it would be possible. Then there had been the fear over losing the baby. She never had a doubt God *could* prevent that from happening, but she wasn't sure He would. Over the years she had seen too many situations where God could have healed someone or prevented something from happening but hadn't. She had no reason to believe He would keep her from losing the baby.

Even now, as she lay there, her hand settled protectively over her abdomen. They weren't completely out of the woods, and even if the doctor said she was, she probably wouldn't believe him until she held the baby in her arms.

Yea, though I walk through the valley of the shadow of death, I will fear no evil: for thou are with me; thy rod and thy staff they comfort me.

The verse from the twenty-third Psalm came to mind. That psalm had been one she had memorized as a young girl in Sunday school. Earlier that day when she'd been so sure she was losing the baby, Laurel realized she had feared evil. She hadn't taken comfort in God's presence regardless of what happened. In fact, she'd been prepared to blame God if the worst had happened. It had just seemed too overwhelming to lose her marriage and then face the prospect of losing her baby within such a short time.

It hadn't all been bad, of course. She had finally been able to claim Rose as her own. But her marriage and the baby still hung in the balance. And fear was the overwhelming emotion she felt where both were concerned. Though she didn't voice it to Matt, there was part of her that wondered if he really had changed, if he could escape the ugliness of his past and be the exception to all the statistics. She wanted proof. But there was no way he could produce that proof. Just like no one could guarantee she would carry this baby safely to term.

Trust in Me, do not put your trust in men. Trust Me.

Though Laurel couldn't remember specific verses, she knew there were many places in the Bible that talked about trusting God instead of trusting man. Why couldn't she trust that God would do what was best for her and the baby? And that He really could free Matt from his past and make him a changed man?

Hot tears burned her cheeks. She was scared. Plain and simple. Scared that what God thought was best for her was different from what she wanted. Could she really put her complete trust in Him in a way she never had before? Trust Him to be there for her regardless of what happened? If she lost the baby, could she trust Him to comfort her and give her peace? If Matt really hadn't changed, could she trust God to be the one that would fulfill all her needs?

Laurel clutched the sheet in her fists. It was easy to trust God when everything was going the way she'd planned for her life. But facing what she'd faced the past few weeks was making her question exactly how strong her faith in God was. When push came to shove, she floundered. It wasn't what she wanted. She wanted her faith to be strong, to be able to trust God in everything.

She pressed her fingers to her eyes. *Please, God, I want to place my trust completely in You. To be able to accept Your plan for my life, whatever that may be. I want my decisions and reactions to reflect You in my life. Help me to remember that You are always with me to comfort and guide me, no matter what happens. I pray You will help Matt and I work through the difficulties we've faced in our marriage recently. Help me to be the kind of wife he needs as he tries to be the husband and father we need him to be. I trust in You.*

"I trust in You," Laurel whispered aloud in the dimly lit room. She felt the fear that had so overwhelmed her begin to fade. And as she lay there, a song from her childhood began to play in her mind. They'd sung lots of hymns in church, and they were the only songs Gran had played on the stereo in the manor. Even though it had been quite a while since she'd last sung the song, the words were all there in her memory.

All the way my Savior leads me, what have I to ask beside? Can I doubt His tender mercy, who through life has been my Guide?

Heav'nly peace, divinest comfort, here by faith in Him to dwell! For I know, whate'er befall me, Jesus doeth all things well; For I know, whate'er befall me, Jesus doeth all things well.

She knew the other verses too, but chose to just softly sing that verse over and over. The last line a poignant reminder of what she'd just come to realize for herself. *For I know, whate'er befall me, Jesus doeth all things well.* The comfort of that knowledge freed her finally from the bondage of fear, and she knew she could trust God with everything that lay ahead for her, Matt, Rose and the baby.

∼ Chapter Nineteen ∽

$\mathbf{T}$HE night before, Laurel hadn't been sure she'd be able to attend church in the morning, but when she woke up she wasn't in too much pain and felt a deep desire to be there. It took her a little longer than usual to get ready, but when she felt presentable, she ventured downstairs.

"You going to church?" Violet asked when she walked into the kitchen.

"Yep. I think I feel good enough to go sit for an hour or so."

"That's great! It's wonderful to see you recovering so quickly," Jessa said as she set a bowl of cereal in front of Rose. "Just remember the service is a little earlier this week as the church goes to summer schedule with no Sunday school."

"Sit down," Violet told her. "And tell me what to get for you."

Laurel started to protest but then settled on a stool at the counter. "Just tea and toast this morning. No morning sickness yet, but I'm not going to tempt it by eating anything too heavy."

Movement in the hallway caught her attention, and she glanced over to see Matt walk into the kitchen. Her mouth went dry at the sight of him in a dark blue plaid shirt that hung open over fitted white T-shirt and jeans that rode low on his hips. His hair still looked damp, no doubt from a shower, and she bet he smelled scrumptious. Her husband was definitely one good looking man.

"Hope this is okay for church," Matt said as he approached the counter. "I didn't really think when I was packing."

"It's fine," Jessa assured him. "Especially now that's it's summer, you'll see a bit of everything."

"Here you go," Violet said as she set a cup of coffee down in front of him.

"Thanks." He turned to look at Laurel. "Are you sure you're up to going?"

Laurel nodded. "I think it will be fine. If all I'd do here is sit around, I can do that just as well at church."

"Sounds good," Matt said with a smile. Though his smile made her stomach flip, it wasn't the smile he usually reserved for her. She hoped they could talk at some point later that day, so she could share with him the revelation she'd had in the night.

Violet set her tea and toast down. "Are you sure that's all you want?"

"Yes. This is perfect. Thank you." She bowed her head to quickly say grace before eating the light breakfast Violet had prepared for her.

Lily showed up a few minutes later, passed on any food, but grabbed a cup of coffee.

"You need to eat something," Jessa said.

Lily shook her head. "I'm not hungry yet. And I think a group of us are going out for lunch, so I'll just eat then."

Laurel saw the concerned frown on Jessa's face and realized the weight her sister must carry since Gran's death. No doubt her own problems had added to the burden Jessa already carried, but she hoped that soon that would no longer be a concern. And in the days to come, maybe she could help take some of the pressure off Jessa, not just with Rose but Lily as well.

In fact, the last few days here at the manor, without Gran's overbearing presence, Laurel had started to think how nice it would be to live closer to her family. As adults and without Gran to stress their relationships, they seemed to get along much better. Well, all except Cami. But maybe this next month would help her see things a bit differently too.

Rose rode to church with her and Matt while Lily went with Jessa and Violet. As they filed into the pew, Rose ended up between Laurel and Jessa while Matt sat on her other side. Dean and Violet also sat with them while Addy went to the junior worship they had for ages seven and under. They nearly filled the pew and drew a few gazes from the people around them.

The music. The sermon. The whole service was just what Laurel needed right then. As she listened to the pastor talk about the people who had trusted God even when what was required of them seemed unthinkable, Laurel realized there was no way to grow in her faith without trust. She'd been drifting along for so many years without any real challenge to how much she trusted and believed in God. That had all changed in the past few weeks. She hoped that even when things got back to a more normal place that she would never again take her faith for granted.

Matt sat stiffly beside her for most the service. Standing when the congregation stood, sitting when they sat. Back when things had been better, when they'd sat together in church, he'd often put his arm around her or at the very least, hold her hand. That he did none of that now, showed just how far they'd drifted from each other.

Because no one was up to cooking, they all decided to hit up one of the restaurants in town. Though none of it was overly taxing, Laurel was nonetheless glad to get home so she could slip away for a little nap. Rose was busy coloring and Matt and Jessa were once again in deep discussion about whatever it was that Jessa wanted for her greenhouse, so she figured it was a good time.

She only slept for about an hour, but it was enough to take the edge off her earlier tiredness. Back downstairs she found the family outside this time. Jessa sat on the porch swing while Dean, Violet, Addy, Rose and Matt played a game of volleyball at the net that had been set up.

"Hey," Jessa said when she spotted her. She patted the swing next to her. "Come sit."

Laurel didn't need to be asked twice. "What a nice afternoon to be outside."

"I know. It's just lovely."

"Mommy!" Laurel watched Rose dart toward the porch, her heart swelling at the name she could now bear proudly.

"Hi, sweetheart," Laurel said with a smile as the girl joined her and Jessa on the swing. "Are you done your game?"

"We're losing," Rose said with a frown.

The others also abandoned the game and joined them on the porch. Matt had taken off his plaid shirt so now he wore just his t-shirt and jeans. His physical strength was more evident in the fitted shirt, but it was a strength born of hard work, not going to the gym.

Right then she wanted nothing more than to be held in his arms, instead she said, "Would you be able to take me to the store?"

His brows drew together. "Are you sure you're up for that?"

She nodded. "Yes, and I need to be walking more anyway."

"Can I come too?" Rose asked.

"Sure," Laurel said. "Do you have something you'd like to buy?"

"I don't know, but I have some allowance left."

"Well, go get it and we'll see what we find at the store."

"Do you need anything, Jessa?" Laurel asked. "I'm going to pick up some more fruits and veggies."

By the time Rose reappeared, Laurel had a few more items on her list. Matt retrieved his shirt from the railing of the porch and went to get his truck keys. Though Laurel knew all the hurdles hadn't been passed yet, she reveled in the feeling of being with her husband and daughter.

After helping Rose find something to buy, they moved to the grocery section of the store. Matt pushed the cart, reaching the things that Laurel needed or having Rose grab things that were at her level. Love swelled in Laurel's heart for her little family as they worked together.

"Can I buy some cookies?" Rose asked as they neared the end of their shopping list.

"*Buy* cookies?" Laurel feigned shock. "I can't even imagine!"

"But you need to rest so you can't make cookies right now." Rose grinned. "Plus, I just love those white ones with the colored frosting and sprinkles."

Unable to resist her daughter's pleading even if she'd wanted to, Laurel nodded. "Okay, just this once. But next time we're going to find a recipe and make them."

"Can I just go get them from the bakery? I know exactly where they are," Rose told her.

"Yep. Meet us at the front by the cash registers, okay? No talking to strangers," Laurel cautioned her.

"I know. Jessa told me that and to yell if anyone tried to touch me."

"Sounds good. Off you go."

"Thanks, Mommy," Rose said before darting away.

As she rounded the end of the aisle, there was suddenly a loud crash and a voice raised in anger. Matt immediately abandoned Laurel and the cart to sprint in the direction Rose had gone. Laurel moved as fast she could to see what had happened.

As she rounded the corner she immediately spotted Matt

standing with Rose pressed to his side, his hand on her shoulder. Rose's eyes were wide with fear. On the floor was a broken jar of pickles.

An elderly woman had lifted her cane to point at Rose and let lose a string of obscenities about reckless children. Laurel froze in place, fear growing in her heart to match that on Rose's face.

Matt's hand came up in a fist, but he didn't swing at the older woman, he just stuck a finger in her direction and said, "Don't you speak like that to my daughter."

"Well, you should teach your hooligan daughter to be more respectful of her elders," the old woman shot back. Then she made a couple of comments regarding Matt's parentage and swore some more.

Laurel could see the anger rising in Matt. His eyes had narrowed as he stared at the woman. "It was an accident. There was absolutely no call for you to speak to her, or anyone for that matter, in that way."

"She charged around that corner without even looking. Pure recklessness. She should be punished." As if to add emphasis to her words, the woman lifted her cane again.

Rose's eyes widened even further and she pressed even more closely against Matt.

"Raise that cane to her one more time and I promise you, I will break it," Matt said, his voice harsh.

A crowd was gathering then, but neither Matt nor the old woman seemed to notice.

"Like daughter, like father, I guess," the woman sneered. "Going around breaking and ruining things, the both of you. My shoes are ruined thanks to her. And now you want to break my cane too? Is that how you treat an older person?"

"Only one who shows that they don't know how to treat other people in general. If you're having a bad day, fine, but don't take it out on a young girl over something that was clearly an accident."

The woman lifted her cane again, but before Matt could

grab it, Laurel stepped in. "We'll pay you for the damage done to your shoes."

The old woman swung toward her. "Who do you think..." If it was possible, the anger already emanating from the woman intensified. "You're a Collingsworth, aren't ya?"

Seeing that level of anger in the woman, Laurel was almost afraid to respond, but she did. "Yes, I'm Laurel Collingsworth."

"Well you and your whole family can just..." Laurel winced as the woman shouted at the top of her lungs where she felt the Collingsworths should go. "You think you can just barge in and take what doesn't belong to you? To ruin everything for people?"

Laurel stared at the woman, dumbfounded. "What are you talking about?"

The woman advanced on her, cane gripped tightly in her hand. "Your grandmother stole him from me. When she couldn't have hers, she took mine. He was supposed to marry me, but instead, the Collingsworths took him and left me with nothing."

The pieces fell into place for Laurel then, explaining to some extent, this woman's bitter attitude toward the world. "Listen, that had nothing to do with me. Just let me pay you for your shoes, and we'll go."

"So you want to sweep me under the carpet, just like your grandmother did?"

This time when she lifted the cane in Laurel's direction, Matt stepped in front of her. The woman hit Matt's arm with it and quick as a wink, Matt grabbed it from her hand. "I'm not going to break this, but only because I won't give you one more thing to hold against this family. You need to step away. I will not have any more of your abuse directed at my wife and daughter."

The woman looked so worked up that Laurel was afraid she was going to have a heart attack on the spot. She opened her purse and pulled out several bills. It was probably far more than the woman's shoes were actually worth, but hopefully enough to defuse this situation for now.

Laurel stepped around Matt and held the money out to the woman. "Please use this to purchase new shoes to replace the ones damaged here."

The woman glared at her with such hatred that it took all Laurel had not to step back from her. The woman reached out and swiped the bills from her hand. Matt held out the cane and she did the same with him.

The store manager had arrived by then and with an apologetic look at Laurel, tried to move the older woman from the scene. Another employee arrived to clean up the mess on the floor, and suddenly it was all over.

Laurel let out a deep breath, feeling as if she'd just been assaulted. She gathered Rose into her arms. "Are you okay, sweetie?"

Looking a bit stunned, Rose nodded, but she appeared to be perilously close to tears. Laurel knew they should get out of the store quickly, but still needed the groceries.

"Why don't you go get the cart," Matt suggested. Then he took Rose's hand. "C'mon, sweetheart. Let's go get your cookies."

As Laurel watched them walk away, she thought her heart would explode with love for them. And she was so proud of how both of them had handled the situation.

⁓ Chapter Twenty ⁓

WHEN they met back at the cash registers, Matt's expression was still grim, but Rose's shell shocked look had disappeared. Though she wasn't as excited as she'd been earlier, she had a smile on her face as she clutched her plastic container of cookies. And Laurel knew she'd buy her those cookies every single day if she wanted, just to see that smile.

The ride back to the manor was made in silence. Laurel was having a hard time reading Matt. There no longer was any anger on his face or showing in his body language, but he was definitely not his usual easygoing self.

Once home, Matt sent them inside while he gathered up the bags of groceries. Laurel made a beeline for the washroom, and when she came out, she heard Rose recounting what had happened at the store.

"He was so mad!" Rose exclaimed.

"Matt?" Jessa asked.

"Yes. That mean old woman made him really mad. And she was really mad too." Rose's shoulders slumped. "I didn't mean to bump into her and break the pickles."

Jessa glanced up and met Laurel's gaze as she walked into

the kitchen. "Everything okay?"

Laurel nodded. "We had a bit of an incident at the store, as I'm sure Rose has told you."

"Were you scared, Rosie?" Jessa asked.

Rose's head nodded. "I thought she was going to hit me with her cane. But Matt wouldn't let her hurt me or Mama." A smile grew on her face until she was beaming. "He told her that I was his daughter. And then he went with me to get my cookies." She laid her hand on the container in front of her and then looked at Laurel. "Is he my daddy now?"

Laurel blinked back tears as she wrapped an arm around Rose's shoulders and pressed her cheek to the little girl's hair. "Yes, I think he is."

"When Matt was really mad were you afraid of him, Rose?" Jessa asked.

Laurel frowned at her sister's continuing questions about Matt.

Rose emphatically shook her head. "Nope. He was mad at that woman, but he didn't hurt her even when she hit him with her cane."

Jessa's eyebrows shot up. "Who was this woman?"

Laurel sighed. "I'm not one hundred percent sure, but from what she yelled at me when she realized I was a Collingsworth, I think she was dating or maybe even engaged to the man Gran ended up marrying."

Jessa rolled her eyes. "Oh yeah. Her. She's taken a strip off me and Gran each time she's run into us. I just got to the point where I avoid her if I see her before she sees me, or just walk away if she does manage to get to me."

"She seems to be a very bitter person."

"I guess I might be too, but she's carried it a bit too far. Especially considering that Gran has tried to make it up to her. I believe she gave the woman some money each month. I know money doesn't make everything better, but Gran felt that the woman had viewed Philip as the way out of the poor life she'd led. So Gran tried to give that to her when she came into control of the Collingsworth fortune. Never made any difference in the woman's attitude apparently."

Laurel shuddered. "Well, I will definitely be steering clear of her in the future!"

"Yep, definitely the best plan of action. We'd better warn Violet about her." Jessa grinned mischievously. "I might just let Cami experience her firsthand however."

Laurel chuckled as she shook her head at Jessa. "How did that woman know who I was anyway?"

"I think she keeps tabs on us somehow. And we're not exactly unknown in this town. If she was at the memorial service, she would have seen all of us."

"True. I'm sure she was there, but I'm surprised she didn't decide to dance in the aisles." Laurel glanced around the kitchen and saw the bags of groceries on the floor. "Where did Matt go?"

Jessa jerked her head in the direction of the back door. "He came in, set them on the floor and walked out."

"Are you okay putting them away?" Laurel asked as she moved toward the door. "I think I need to talk to him."

"I'm fine. Rose will help me, right?"

Laurel heard Rose agree as she pushed open the back door. Her only purpose then was finding her husband.

〜∞∞〜

Matt bent and picked another stone from the rocky beach. With a flick of his wrist, he sent it skipping across the water. Though right then he'd much rather have been hitting a punching bag with his fists, this was all he'd allow himself. Vestiges of his early anger still burned in him. When he'd grabbed that old woman's cane earlier, it had taken everything within him to not return the hit she'd given him. He had also wanted to punch her in the mouth to get her to stop spewing her venom around Rose.

He supposed he should just be glad he hadn't carried through, but it still made him feel lower than low that he'd even had those thoughts about the woman.

Be angry, and do not sin. The words of a verse Devon had quoted to him when he'd come to see him floated into his mind. Devon had told him that anger in and of itself was not a sin, that even Jesus had experienced anger. But the key was to not sin even as he was experiencing it.

Matt shoved his hands into his pockets and bent his head. He was pretty sure that while his actions hadn't been a sin, his thoughts toward the woman had been.

"Forgive me, Lord. I shouldn't have thought what I did about her. Please continue to help me with this. I want to get better. I want to be the husband and father Laurel, Rose and this baby need me to be."

"Matt?"

At the sound of his wife's voice, Matt lifted his head and turned around. His heart skipped a beat when he saw Laurel. She stood where the path from the manor's back yard ended and the rocky beach began, her hands clasped in front of her. Slowly she made her way across the rocks to where he stood.

She looked up at him, concern on her face. "Are you okay?"

Matt turned his gaze back to the lake. "I will be. I'm sorry for what happened at the store."

Laurel laid a hand on his arm, but didn't say anything until he looked back at her. "What are you sorry for? You didn't do anything wrong."

"I allowed the anger to take over," he said.

Laurel's lips curved into a small smile. "The woman walked out of there with all her body parts still attached and no bruises, so I'd say that you did a pretty good job of controlling it."

Matt didn't answer right away, but then said, "You think so? Fortunately, you don't know what was going through my mind."

"Probably the same thing that was going through mine," Laurel commented drily. "I really wanted the woman to stop swearing at Rose and was almost to the point of physically making that happen. I was angry too."

Matt shook his head. "It was just a bad scene all the way around."

"Rose was telling Jessa all about it when I came out of the bathroom."

With a sigh, Matt bent his head and rubbed a hand across his face. "Was she scared?"

"She told Jessa that you were really mad. And Jessa asked her if she was scared, and she said yes."

"Oh man. I'm sorry. I didn't mean to scare her."

Laurel shook her head. "She wasn't scared of you. She thinks you're the greatest."

Matt looked up, his brow furrowed. "She thinks I'm the greatest?"

"You bet. First of all you protected her from that awful woman. That's what made her scared. Not you."

"First? There's more?"

Laurel reached out to take his hand in hers. She felt tears prick her eyes again as she said, "Second, and what made her absolutely glow when she told Jessa, was that you told that woman that Rose was your daughter."

For a moment, Matt stood speechless. His heart pounded within his chest. He remembered saying the words and in that moment they had never felt more true. For all intents and purposes, Rose was his daughter.

Laurel seemed to understand his inability to speak in that moment. She smiled up at him, laying her hand on the side of his face. "And finally, she adores you because you took her to get her cookies."

Matt tried to laugh, but it kind of came out as a strangled sob. He wrapped his arms around Laurel and pulled her close against him. Though he wasn't one given to tears, and in fact couldn't remember the last time he'd shed any, they flowed now. Laurel's arms wrapped tightly around his waist, and for the first time in months, Matt felt real hope stirring within him.

"Do you think we can make this work, babe?" he asked as he stared across the top of Laurel's head at the lake with tear blurred vision.

Laurel moved back a bit and he looked back to see her regarding him with a smile. "Yes, I know we can. I have been struggling to trust God with the baby, you and our marriage. Last night He and I came to an understanding, or rather, He opened my mind to understand what trusting Him is really all about. So we will take this one day at a time, and trust God to help us over any rough spots, knowing He won't forsake us should things get rough."

"Are you sure?" Matt's voice was barely a rough whisper. "I thought I'd lost you."

"I am very sure," Laurel said. "We're not just going to get through this, we're going to rock this parent thing, and I think our marriage is gonna be stronger than ever." Laurel placed a hand on either side of his head and drew him down so their lips met. After a few gentle kisses, she said, "I've missed you."

"I've missed you too," Matt replied and then returned to the very enjoyable act of kissing the love of his life.

When he pulled back a short time later, they were both a little breathless. He winked at her and asked, "Think they'll miss us if we just hang here for a bit and make out a little?"

Laurel gave him a flirtatious look that he hadn't seen in so long that his heart began to pound at an alarming rate. "Hey, we're married, so it's allowed."

As Matt led her to the swing and drew her down carefully onto his lap, he said a prayer of thanks that God had guided them through these past few weeks to a place that was even better than he could ever have imagined. Though it had been a painful journey, for the first time in years, Matt felt truly free of his past. And he realized now that true freedom didn't come from hiding what had happened all those years ago like he thought it would. It had come from bringing it all out in the open for Laurel and others to see. Now the true process of healing could begin, and Matt knew that God had brought them through the fire to purify and strengthen their faith in Him and their love for each other.

"I love you, Laurel," Matt murmured against her lips.

Laurel moved back just a bit and smiled at him. "I'm glad, because I love you too, and can't wait to move onto this next chapter in our lives." She placed his hand against her stomach. "This little one and Rose will complete the parts of our family we didn't even know were missing. I'm just glad that God revealed His plan for us, even when we already had planned out what we thought we wanted for our lives."

Matt held Laurel close and with his foot set the swing in motion. He had seen beauty rise from the ashes of his marriage that day. He'd been so sure it was all over between them, but now not only did he have his marriage back, it was back stronger than it had ever been. For that, and so many other things, he was grateful to God. Though there were still some unknowns ahead of them, he felt confident God was going before them and would prepare them for whatever lay ahead. That knowledge gave him a peace he'd never had before.

༄❦

As Laurel rested her head on Matt's shoulder, she let out a long, contented sigh. The place, at that moment, was perfection for her. Even knowing the challenges that could still face them, Laurel knew there was nowhere else she'd rather be but in her husband's arms. They would face all trials together and with God's help, they would overcome them.

The peacefulness of the lake washed over her, and for the first time in her life, the manor truly felt like a home, a place of love. She would forever remember that this was the place where she and Matt had experienced healing for their past hurts and found their way back to each other.

She hoped Matt was right and that Gran really had planned this month ahead for them to heal their relationships as sisters. Already she could see it happening, and Laurel hoped that once Cami arrived, they would all be able to come together in love in the home that had once brought so much heart ache. No matter where they went in the world, she hoped that this would always be the place they would come home to. She knew that for her and Matt this would be their home away from home. The place where their family had grown, and their love had been reborn.

‹› *The End* ‹›

OTHER TITLES AVAILABLE BY

Kimberly Rae Jordan
(Christian Romances)

Marrying Kate

Faith, Hope & Love

Waiting for Rachel (*Those Karlsson Boys: 1*)
Worth the Wait (*Those Karlsson Boys: 2*)
The Waiting Heart (*Those Karlsson Boys: 3*)

Home Is Where the Heart Is (*Home to Collingsworth: 1*)
Home Away From Home (*Home to Collingsworth: 2*)
Love Makes a House a Home (*Home to Collingsworth: 3*)
The Long Road Home (*Home to Collingsworth: 4*)
Her Heart, His Home (*Home to Collingsworth: 5*)
Coming Home (*Home to Collingsworth: 6*)

A Little Bit of Love:
A Collection of Christian Romance Short Stories

For more details on the availability of these titles,
please go to

www.KimberlyRaeJordan.com

Contact

Please visit Kimberly Rae Jordan on the web!
Website: www.kimberlyraejordan.com
Facebook: www.facebook.com/AuthorKimberlyRaeJordan
Twitter: twitter.com/Kimberly Jordan

49416170R00116

Made in the USA
Middletown, DE
15 October 2017